Hands of Chaos

Book 3 of the Shady Woods series

J Mercer

Published 2022 in the United States of America by Bare Ink

Hardcover ISBN: 978-1-7348883-8-6

Paperback ISBN: 979-8-9872567-0-1

Ebook ISBN: 9781734888393

Library of Congress Control Number: TXu002221752

HANDS OF CHAOS / written by J Mercer

Cover design by Jim Mayfield

Copy edits by Katharine Lamoureaux

Contents

To Brie, for that Shady Woods ornament you made me so long ago
and your never-ending excitement for what I create

Chapter One

Rabbit Holes

The Sentinel were imposing, dressed in black from head to toe, which helped them slip in and out of the shadows. Their special issue "Take back your pride!" lanyards made them seem like they were fighting something, when they were just supposed to be keeping wayward strangers out of Shady Woods.

Though I could see the point of them, in theory, I didn't like them in practice. Three currently stood in the middle of the road, down past the blood bank. The road was cleared of snow, which was piled high on the curbs, and stray holiday decorations were still strung from the town's street lamps. From here, a block away, I could see a large stain of animal blood beneath their feet, leftover from the last full moon.

"You okay, Grace?" Riah asked, yanking me from my thoughts as my friends filed inside the Silver Subs building.

With a deep breath of the icy January air, I followed. "I don't know. Am I?"

He smirked and drew in a deep breath. His wolf ability to smell emotion was like having an inside look at me, which was frustrating only because I couldn't do the same. As a dendrite, I could speak directly into someone's mind, maybe flood them with feelings and place a thought once in a while, but I couldn't read minds or poke around in them.

I knew if Christian hadn't been there, reaching his hand back for mine, that Riah would have moved closer, not that he couldn't read me just fine from where he was. "Apprehension, mistrust, and disapproval, to name a few."

"I don't like the Sentinel," I explained.

"Justin's a Sentinel."

It felt like needle pricks, hearing my brother linked to them. He'd graduated last year and I was still reeling from his decision not to go to college, even if most of the Shady residents didn't. The town operated more on an internship and family business basis, since there were very few communities like ours where above normals—abnormals for short—chose to peacefully coexist. Definitely none with colleges. But my brother and I had been raised to go to college. This hadn't always been my life.

My parents had grown up in Shady, moved to Chicago for college, and raised my brother and I there until my thoughts broke into some random cashier's head. Unfortunately, this cashier was part of the Hand of Humanity, and that was all it took for her to commit herself to eradicating me and my family. We escaped back here so I could better learn to control myself and to avoid the sticky situation of having to kill her before she killed us.

Regardless of my thoughts on college, and my original assumptions that Justin and I would live normal as adults, Justin had announced that he and his girlfriend Clara were going to join the Sentinel. He was going to marry her and never leave Shady, so if he eventually wanted a degree, he'd do it online. Clara was a vampire and it was hardest for vampires who wanted a normal life to live anywhere else—hard to find a blood bank willing to regularly sell a private citizen a gallon unless you were in Shady Woods, Wisconsin.

Stella ordered the cold clam chowder, Ethan a steaming mug of warm sustenance, as he put it, and Riah requested his sub meaty and raw, no veggies or sauce.

I ordered turkey, as did Christian, my mostly dendrite, somewhat siren boyfriend.

Christian waited for our subs while the rest of us grabbed a table, but as I walked past Nehemiah's booth and caught sight of his bashed in face, I stopped right there in front of him to gawk. Not very cool of me, I know.

Everyone considered Nehemiah and his friends to be trouble, but considering the tear-your-throat-out, disregard-of-human-life trouble, you'd think a few kids who liked to skip class wouldn't be a huge problem. In the few years I'd been around, I'd never seen any other sign they'd gotten in a fight. Besides, it wasn't *they* who'd gotten in a fight—Preston and Reilly looked just fine.

Preston noticed me first, then Reilly. When Nehemiah finally looked up from his sandwich—werewolves were that attached to food—he grinned, even winked.

"Like what you see?" he asked. Reilly snickered. Preston looked down at his sub.

"Sorry, I just..."

"Haven't seen anyone so handsome before?"

One eye was puffy and sealed shut, the other more purple than I could have imagined a bruise to be. He had thin scabs on his forehead and chin, rug burns almost, or like maybe his face had been pressed into the street.

I sat down next to him, as if acting like we were friends who sat next to each other could excuse my ogling. "What happened?"

"I like to explore and the Sentinel don't take kindly to that."

"I like to explore, too," Preston said, motioning to his un-marred face. "What they don't take kindly to is his mouth."

Werewolves were the strongest of us. By a long shot. Nehemiah's knuckles, however, were perfectly neat. "Did you not defend yourself?"

"I didn't." He beamed. "Wanna kiss the bruises?"

Christian appeared, subs in hand, and cleared his throat at that. Nehemiah snickered.

"Why wouldn't you defend yourself?" I asked.

"So there was something to report to the police. Something to document."

I frowned. "That's..."

"Brilliant? Yeah, you're welcome."

Christian nudged me, nodding toward our table. I stood, not sure what else to say, how to leave it. Christian left, slid into our booth, and as I turned away, Nehemiah caught my hand.

"Grace, right?"

I nodded. He let go and got back to his sandwich.

"This is a problem," I said as I sat down. "The Sentinel are a problem."

Stella shrugged both thin shoulders, Ethan took a drink, Christian muttered how Nehemiah was the problem, and Riah slid a newspaper across the table.

A real newspaper. Because Shady news didn't make it online in case any conspiracy theorists might figure it for the truth. The headline on the front page read "We've lost sight of where we've been." It was an op-ed piece on what the new town council had been up to since November, when purists had nearly swept the election.

Purist: an abnormal who thinks we should all live by instinct. Outside of Shady Woods, this meant vampires drinking fresh from whatever human or dendrite they might come across, and werewolves tearing into whatever flesh they might happen by on a full moon. Inside Shady, it started a movement to stay locked in our homes that one night a month so the wolves didn't have to travel to find an unpopulated area of wilderness.

The article outlined how the new council was not following all the founding tenets of Shady Woods. Riah was touchy about the whole situation because his dad was one of only two original council members left. That meant five were purists, we had the Sentinel watching our borders, and Riah thought everything meant something.

I turned to Christian. "You think Nehemiah deserved that? You think anyone could deserve that?"

"I think he should keep his hands off you."

Rolling my eyes to Riah, I said it again. "The Sentinel are a problem."

"I'm more worried about Hollywood."

I snorted. "That's cute."

"No, I'm serious. Look at this." Unlocking his phone, he opened it up to a website and set it down on top of the paper. "A bunch of celebrities didn't show for the film awards."

Christian peered at it. "That's just gossip."

"It's national news. One producer made a joke about them being werewolves, because it was the full moon, but what if it's true?"

"How many of them?" I asked, always willing to go a little further down Riah's rabbit hole than the others.

"Three."

Stella turned his phone toward her and started reading, her strawberry-blonde hair falling like water around her face when she dipped her head.

"They probably just flaked." Ethan wiped a drop of blood off the edge of his mug. "They're celebrities."

"Two of them were supposed to present the lifetime achievement award. You don't bail on that unless you have to."

"It says right here Cynthia Jackson had the flu, Glinda Rae needed a mental health day, which—and I quote 'is not abnormal for her'—and J.D. Sanger, well, he can do pretty much whatever he wants, can't he?" Stella looked up at Riah.

"Why would this friend say"—he snatched his phone from her and scrolled back up—"J.D. was planning to be there. I talked to him when he was getting ready. I don't know what happened."

"Okay," I agreed. "It's fishy."

Christian rolled his eyes. He thought I humored Riah too much. Then again, he thought I everything-ed Riah too much ."If they were werewolves, they wouldn't have agreed to present on the full moon in the first place."

"Unless they didn't know they were going to be werewolves when they agreed," Riah said. "What if someone just turned them?"

"All of them at once?" Ethan asked.

Stella tilted her head. "Three celebrities isn't really laying low."

"Particularly if you know it's going to cut into the awards," Christian agreed.

"I'm not saying whoever did it was trying to lay low."

We stared at Riah, deciding collectively without discussing it that he was taking it one step too far, then went back to our sandwiches.

Christian put an arm around me. "You sure you don't want to come to Emily's party?"

"I'm sure I'm not invited." Her birthday party was tonight. A sleepover, on a Sunday.

"But do you want to come?"

I tossed him a grin. "Not one bit." Though Aster was one of my best friends, and Jeremy and Kevin liked me enough, Sofia and Emily hated me with everything in them. The feeling was mutual, and not because Sofia was Christian's ex-girlfriend, but because they were simply awful.

"I'm not really comfortable going to a sleepover without you," he said.

"Then don't."

"We always go to each other's birthdays. It's been a thing since like second grade. Come with me."

"My parents would never let me stay over. Not on a school night. Even if I went, I'd have to be home by ten."

"Sofia and Emily have school night sleepovers all the time."

"My parents don't care what Sofia and Emily do."

"Please?"

"Never," I told him. "But I love you."

He sighed, because he felt I used those words as an apology more than anything, or to soften the delivery of something I knew he didn't want to hear. He got out of the booth and knocked his knuckles on the table. *You always pick Riah after the full moon.*

I leveled a warning look at him. I was not going to have this conversation again. Kiara always slept for a few days after the full moon, so it was the best time to spend with Riah unless I wanted to spend time with Kiara too. Which I did not. Regardless, I wouldn't have gone to this party with him. *Riah has zero to do with it.*

I really think you should be there, Grace.

I'm not welcome, and my parents wouldn't let me. I'm going to Ethan's.

Ethan turned to nuzzle Stella, which he often did when he felt we were holding a silent conversation, one dendrite mind to another. It was rude of us, but nearly impossible not to once in a while, when you could.

Christian's lips pressed tight while he rubbed at the crystal strung around his neck—the crystal he'd bought to help him make sense of his dreams, which were known to be portent.

Did you have a dream you didn't tell me about? I asked.

He shook his head, but it seemed more like a sad, disappointed shake than an actual answer. Then, with one more knock on the table, he left.

Chapter Two

That's a Big Fat No

There was a strange woman sitting on Ethan's porch.

It was January in northern Wisconsin, so sitting on the porch was odd enough, but Ethan's brother Eric sat there too. He was turned away from her, nearly in the shrub and pressed up against the wrought iron rail, his long vampire form stiff, knees pointing in the opposite direction.

Stella careened into the curb in front of their house, which was how she usually came to a complete stop. Ethan stumbled out of her car and over the short snowbank. He stopped there to gape. As I pulled into my driveway next door, Riah got out of my car and walked around it, but didn't move across the lawn. He waited, eyes on Ethan to see what he would do.

What's the problem? I asked Riah silently. Ethan was so still, I couldn't be sure he was breathing. He and the woman stared at each other. *Who is she?*

But Ethan was moving now, so Riah was too. He was far enough from me that if he answered, I didn't hear it.

She was stretched thin, which I could see even with her folded on the steps the way she was. Definitely a wild vampire—wild implying she lived on the outskirts of society or in the wilderness, often moving to not draw attention to the bodies in her wake. It was how the majority of vampires and wolves lived. Her curly black hair was cut jaggedly at her shoulders, and her cheeks were sunken holes under grossly protruding cheekbones. Chin smudged with dirt. Hair in tangles. Sweatshirt: frayed at the collar. Puffy coat: holes on both elbows. From inside it all, she smiled up at Ethan as we approached.

"Hi, baby."

"Hi, Mom."

My eyes about bugged out of my head.

"Surprise," Eric muttered.

"Riah." She nodded at him.

"Mrs. Parrino." He nodded back.

Her gaze skipped over Stella and back to Ethan. "Is this your girlfriend?"

"Yes."

"Nice to meet you, son's girlfriend." She held out her hand.

Stella took it. "Nice to meet you, too."

Mrs. Parrino looked at the boys. "You three have grown up quite nice."

"Save it," Eric spit.

"Maybe not politely, but nice," she amended. "Eric won't ask me in." This she directed to her youngest son.

"What are you doing here?" Ethan's face had hardened into a blank sheet of ice, and I realized that no matter how many times I'd thought his cool, calm, collected vampire expression had been emotionless, it had never been like this. This was either an effective mask or complete lack of concern.

"For starters, I could use a shower."

"I don't think the current Mrs. Parrino would like you using our shower," Ethan said.

"Don't be silly. I'm not back to take her husband away."

"Then what are you back for?" Eric asked, finally looking at her.

She sighed. "I know you don't think it's true, but I love you boys. I miss you."

"You could've called."

"I visited once."

"Six years ago."

"This isn't the life I wanted and your father wouldn't let me take you with. What was I to do?" She waved her hand. "Can't we forget the past and catch up?"

"No." Eric stood and walked inside, slamming the door behind him.

"Wanted?" Ethan asked. "Meaning you've changed your mind?"

"I can't be sure yet, but I am a bit tired. When the council invited us to see what it might be like to meld our ways of life, I thought, who better to bring a group in? I know the town, I can show everyone around and introduce them, see my boys, see if I might be ready to settle down."

"The council invited?" Riah echoed, as if this was something he hadn't known.

She nodded and I studied him. If he didn't know, then that meant his dad didn't know. And if his dad didn't know, that meant the new council members were making decisions and taking action without including the old.

"I'm Violet Parrino." The woman held a hand out to me, as if I hadn't put it together yet.

"Grace James," I replied.

She glanced between us. "You're Riah's girlfriend?"

"No," we said at once.

"I think you should go, Mom." Ethan stepped off the narrow front walk to give her clear passage.

"If neither of you will let me in, I'll wait for your dad."

The front door opened and the newer Mrs. Parrino peeked her head out. "Violet!"

"Steff!" Violet stood with a delighted grin and the two women embraced.

When they backed up, they held onto each other's arms as if they were old friends. "It's good to see you," Steff said. "Eric told me you wanted a shower?"

Violet smiled bigger. "Oh, yes."

"Come on in. You know where everything is."

Ethan glared at his stepmom.

She scolded him with a look and the two women headed inside.

Ethan shoved the door open so it smacked against the doorstop, bouncing back into Riah. We followed him to the basement where Eric was sulking. Eric usually didn't join us in the basement, rather keeping to his room, but his room was maybe too close to his mother at the moment.

"I thought your mom..." Died. I thought she'd died. In the few photos they had of her, she looked like a dendrite. And considering their stepmom was a dendrite as well, I'd just assumed. "I thought she was a dendrite."

"She was," Ethan replied.

"She was a dendrite who"—how had she put it?—"wanted a wild's way of life?" I couldn't wrap my mind around it.

"She wanted to live longer," Ethan said. "To feel invincible."

"Which was more important than her kids," Eric added.

I blinked at him. Here I'd been most disgusted with the thought of being a vampire, and she'd chosen it.

Stella wrapped her arms around Ethan's neck and kissed his cheek.

I turned to Riah, wanting more but realizing it wasn't really the time to poke at them. *You knew her? What's the story?*

He didn't even look at me, his hand caught in his sandy brown hair, lifting it up out of his eyes. "The new council campaigned on recreating Shady as a haven, but to flat out ask wilds in?" Slipping his phone out of his pocket, he pulled up his dad's number to message him.

Ethan squinted at me across the coffee table. "She wanted my dad to turn her and he wouldn't—"

"He doesn't believe in turning people," Eric interrupted.

"—so she found someone who would."

Eric stood. "I'm getting out of here. Call me when she's gone, okay?"

Ethan nodded and Eric raced up the stairs. I took Riah's phone from him to start some music, something Ethan usually did the moment he walked down the stairs.

Riah's dad replied that he'd been told the wilds were coming. That they'd reached out to request safe harbor. Riah leaned forward, elbows to his knees, and took a deep breath in.

We sat in silence for a bit, Ethan's favorite playlist pulsing around us, our minds whirling in different directions, until the door at the top of the stairs opened and his mother appeared in clothes of his stepmom's that I recognized. They were too short on her, the sleeves and the pants, but hung baggy. Stepping off the stairs, she moved along the wall, studying the pictures on the ledge and asking after the people she found in them.

Ethan filled her in, short and sweet, and soon she was clutching a picture of her and Eric and Ethan.

"Think your dad would let me have this one?" she asked.

"You say that like you plan to leave again."

"I don't have any plans. Haven't had plans in ten years, really." She unclenched her fingers from the frame and set it back on the shelf. "I do have dinner plans, though. Thought maybe you'd come meet my friends and help me show them around."

"Yeah, that's a big fat no."

She sighed, patting the shelf where her hand lingered. "Think about it. Maybe we could all have dinner sometime."

Ethan snorted. His mom took a deep breath in, and with a decisive nod, headed back up the stairs.

"I'd have dinner with them," I offered.

"Of course you would." Riah muttered. "You'd also square off with a wild vampire who had blood running down his face if I let you."

I rolled my eyes to him. "I'm much more prepared for such a standoff now, thank you very much." He was referring to a few years ago when I was still mouthy and didn't appreciate my vulnerability as much as he would have liked.

"You're much more prepared for a standoff with a wolf," he pointed out. "Not a wild vampire."

Pursing my lips, I texted Aster, who'd been training me for a while now. After telling her what was going on, I asked her if maybe it was time I started sparring with a vampire.

Not that they were a threat, the ones who'd come to town. They'd asked for safe harbor. That being said, the wilds I'd met so far in my life hadn't been very trustworthy. If wild vampires were going to be swarming town, it couldn't hurt to learn better how to protect myself.

Chapter Three

Done and Done

Christian was very quiet on the way to school the next morning while I babbled on about Ethan's mom and the wilds in town.

As he pulled into the parking lot, I turned to him. "Sorry. I haven't asked about the party."

"Don't ask about the party," he muttered as he got out of the car.

"Was it fun?" I hurried to catch up to him. His legs were longer than mine, but normally he slowed to meet my pace.

"Of course it wasn't fun. You have fun with Riah?"

Stopping to cross my arms, I asked, *You're mad because I was with Riah and Ethan and Stella and Ethan's mom?*

I'm not mad. But he wasn't slowing down either. In fact, he might not have even realized he'd left me behind in the parking lot.

What are you then? I asked.

Scared of losing you.

And though we shared a locker, I couldn't find him in the hall. *Christian, what are you talking about? Where are you?*

But he was gone, and after that, the silence in my head was deafening. I slid into Spanish where Aster sat with Sofia. Since she and Kevin broke up last summer, Aster split her time more neatly between Sofia and I. She sat with me in trig and for lunch, but with Sofia in Spanish and abnormal history.

I shared one of my best friends with the nastiest girl in town. I tried not to think too much about it.

What happened last night? I asked her, but she sat in the front row. Sofia liked to sit in the front row, and Aster couldn't very well text me or pass a note from the front row, so I settled for chewing on my pen.

I hurried to catch up with Aster after class, grabbing her sleeve, and as if Sofia could sense me, she turned around and winked. Along with the wink came the biggest smile I'd ever seen from her. Then the current of students swallowed her up.

"What happened last night?" I asked again.

"Nothing. What do you mean?"

"Sofia just looked at me like she knew my biggest secret."

"You don't have secrets. What's your biggest secret?"

I stared at her. "I don't know."

We ping-ponged from her locker to mine—Christian still nowhere to be found—then made our way to trig where Stella was waiting for us.

During trig, I chewed on my lip instead of my pen, while Aster scribbled possible secrets of mine into her notebook:

You have three nipples.

You didn't actually come from Chicago but are a robot.

You pee your pants at night.

I'm serious. Christian is avoiding me.

Okay okay. I'll ask her next hour.

Next hour for me was English with Riah and Ethan, and I stared at my phone for a straight ten minutes. It sat in my lap as the ellipses told me Aster was working on a text. But nothing came through. Each minute that passed filled me with a greater sense of dread, because the longer it took her to figure out how to say it, the more certain I was that I wouldn't want to hear it.

Maybe it was just hard to type in the front row without getting caught by the teacher.

But then, the fact that she was typing from the front row in the first place also implied I wouldn't want to hear it.

Except, would she type something awful or wait to tell me in person?

Riah sat behind me—English was alphabetical—and I soon felt his fingers on my shoulder. "You okay?" he whispered. Yeah, I was sure I stunk. I tried to rein the worry back in.

No. Waiting for bad news.

"Bad news about what?"

"Riah Jenkins." Mrs. Smith tilted her nose down to look at him above her glasses. "Are you not reading along with us?"

He held up his open copy of *Interview with a Vampire* for her to see. "I most certainly am."

"Please continue then."

His low groan made me smile, and I tried to focus on his voice, which was deep and soothing. She had me read next, and by the time I could have answered his question, I'd forgotten he asked it. Plus, we stopped reading to discuss Armand's theater, where vampires pretended to be mortals pretending to be vampires, and what Anne Rice was trying to say with that.

Aster must have waited to hit send until the bell rang, because her text showed up as I was walking out of class.

Sofia says he made out with Emily last night. I don't really believe it. I'll ask Jeremy if he saw anything.

Spit got caught in my throat. Besides the fact that Christian didn't like Emily much, he was crazy about me. Too crazy, if anything. Jealous, often. I flung open our locker and stared at our books, trying to hold the tears back as they flooded my eyes.

It didn't make any sense.

But then it did. Why he'd been so desperate for me to come with last night. He must have had a dream about it.

I hurried to history so I could catch him before he walked into class, since he'd been avoiding our locker.

Avoiding me.

Why else would he avoid me? The more the seconds ticked by, the more it seemed like the only thing that added up. But also, it made zero sense.

As soon as he came into sight, I blurted out, *Did you think the only way to stop it was if I went to the party with you?* I should be able to reach his mind no matter where he was in the school, but if I could see him, he couldn't pretend he didn't hear me.

He stopped cold, the color draining from his face.

If that wasn't an answer, I didn't know what was.

Spinning on my heel, choking on belief, I walked away as quickly as I could. Past Emily and Sofia, smirking at me, and past Riah, his eyebrows furrowed as he realized I was headed in the wrong direction. My breath was short and shallow. I'd never been so angry.

Grace! Wait!

The bell rang and we stood on opposite ends of the hall.

Now you're willing to talk to me? I asked, furious. Furiously trying not to cry.

We can get through this.

Get through what? I want to hear you say it.

He shook his head, and I could tell his lip was trembling from where I stood. *I can't. I can't say it. I can hardly come to terms with it.*

I scoffed, not that he could hear it. *Poor baby. I feel so bad for what you're going through. Is there something I could do to make this easier for you?*

Now isn't the time for sarcasm.

What is it the time for?

I don't know. Just, let me explain.

I laughed out loud at that. And before he could see my lip start to tremble, I hurried around the corner.

I can't help what I dream! he called after me.

You can help what you do. I wanted the furthest bathroom. But no. First, I wanted him out of my locker. Backtracking, I dumped his books on the floor, shoved mine in, and locked it. We never locked it. I was sure he hadn't memorized the combination.

Then I found the furthest bathroom and chose the furthest stall, to be as far from everyone as I could get. I stared at the Aster's text. And the ones from her pinging through now, about why I wasn't in class and Christian's face was all scrunched up and was I okay and it couldn't be true.

It's true, I typed.

Because it was. It was all that made sense, honestly. He had a dream, begged me to come to the party—thinking my presence would stop it from happening—then chose to go by himself anyway, even though he knew Emily was going to try something. Which, fine. He still could have avoided it, the same way he avoided me all day. He'd had a heads up. All he had to do was keep her an arm's length away and there would have been zero kissing.

Made out, Aster had said. Making out implied intent and duration of time. Making out was not an accident.

Why'd you go? I asked him from my bathroom stall, embarrassed at how small my voice sounded in my head. *If you thought this was unavoidable, why even go to the party?*

You picked Riah.

I did not pick Riah. There were a million reasons for me not to go to that party that had nothing to do with Riah.

It was a dream, Grace. Inevitable. Fate.

What an idiot. *When you dreamt I was taken to the moon last year and bit by a wolf, was I taken to the moon? Was I bit by a wolf?*

He didn't answer. And the longer he didn't answer, the more I cried. Gulps and sniffles and snot and tissue blows and that gasp-gasp-gasp thing you do when you try to catch your breath in the midst of uncontrollable sobs.

When the bell rang for lunch, Christian asked where I was. *Can we talk about this in person?*

The nice thing about speaking in someone's mind is you could do it while sobbing and they couldn't tell. *If you care anything for me, you'll leave me alone.*

If I care anything for you? How can you even say that?

I can say that because we've been together for more than a year and you KISSED SOMEONE ELSE.

Grace. He sent it to me, my name, cracked and broken. *Please.*

Muffled conversation on the other side of the bathroom door, in the hall, distracted me. I took a deep breath and tried to get ahold of myself so whoever it was wouldn't hear me sobbing when they walked in. When the door swung open, I held my breath, hoping they'd leave. Instead, they hopped up on the counter, crinkled a paper bag, and turned on a faucet.

I hung my head low between my legs, making sure to hold my hair so it wouldn't fall on the filthy floor. I had more tears to wring out of me before I could face the rest of the day. Hell if I would miss another class. I wouldn't give Emily or Sofia or Christian the satisfaction of going home because of this.

"It's just us," Stella chimed softly over the noise of the sink, at the same time a text with heart emojis and sinks and toilets came from Aster. "Pretend we're not here."

The tears came fresh with the relief of her voice, and when the desperation to cry it out finally subsided, I blew my nose and walked out of the stall.

"Hey, babe," Aster said, as if nothing had happened. As if we did this every day.

"Want some lunch?" Stella asked, offering me a giant pretzel from the hot lunch line.

I shook my head and leaned up against the counter with my back to the mirror, unable to face what I must look like at the moment.

Aster reached a hand out to touch my shoulder. "Want a hug?"

"No." Hugs would most definitely send me back down the spiral.

The cool breeze of Stella's siren charm wafted over me. Her charm felt slightly different every time, and I wondered if that was her, or if it was dependent on what I needed or how it reacted to whatever I was feeling in the moment. Today it made me feel heavy, but in a stabilizing way.

"Want to talk about it?" she asked.

"No," I said weakly. "I just need to get through the day." Turning to look at myself in the mirror, I visibly recoiled.

"Might we have some silver magic, please?" Aster held her finger out to Stella, who leaned over and dropped a few siren tears onto it. Dabbing at the waving silver ball with her ring finger, Aster blotted the goo gently under my lashes and onto my red nose.

"Close your eyes," she instructed.

The rest she smoothed into my puffy eyelids, then took my shoulders and turned me back to the mirror.

"Tada!"

I watched as the last bit of the tear's sheen faded away. Raw siren tears healed, I knew that, but I wouldn't have thought to use them for something like this. It was odd, looking whole but feeling in shattered pieces.

Stella hopped off the counter. "You ready to do this?"

Aster linked her arm through mine and squeezed, her way of giving me the hug I'd declined. "Riah's waiting outside," she said.

"Ethan's probably pacing by our lockers."

"Everyone knows?"

They didn't answer, which was probably better than having to hear it out loud. Of course everyone knew. Sofia and Emily had surely told anyone who'd listen. And since people tended to hang on their every word...

I pushed through the door and Riah spun toward us. He looked mostly calm and collected, but I knew him well enough to note the tension in his jaw. Yeah, definitely not calm and collected. Me either.

Without a word, we walked back to my locker. Ethan was indeed pacing in front of it, and there was no sign of Christian's littered books beneath it. I didn't speak as I got my things and headed to class.

Physics was easy enough because Stella kept up a steady allotment of charm, and gym was fine because Riah's presence soothed me at least 25%. Plus, we were playing floor hockey, and I threw myself into checking people like I never had before.

The problem was skills. Christian and I had been skills partners since day one of freshman year. It would have been fine if we were still working on fogging, but we were in the middle of placing thoughts. It was more communication than I was up for, so I practiced blocking my mind while picking at my nails until they were red and inflamed, until one started to bleed. Then I watched it bleed, all to keep my mind off the person sitting next to me.

The one person I could feel without looking. The one mind I could sense without trying.

I closed my eyes and bit my lip, then pushed the tip of my pencil into my leg. Taking in a steadying breath, I let it out slowly. When I felt in control again and opened my eyes, Mr. Turner was nearby, studying me. He was always about steering us back on task when it seemed we weren't doing what we were supposed to be doing, so I sent him a look that said, as best I could, *sometimes life really sucks for teenagers, and I could use a pass today.*

However the look translated, he walked by with only a pat on my shoulder.

When the bell rang, Christian blurted out, "Can I drive you home?"

I looked at him like he was an idiot, then remembered that he was. He was an idiot and an asshole. What a paradigm shift. "No."

"Can I come over?"

Scooping up my books, I stood. "For what?"

"To talk."

"We have nothing to talk about."

"We can fix this, Grace."

"We are one hundred percent not fixing this." And I looked at him. Really looked at him, so he could feel it, how serious I was. "We are done."

Chapter Four

You're Perfect

I wish I could say I bounced back from the Christian and Emily situation like a champ, but I spent a fair amount of time moping.

Riah decided running would help this, and Aster pushed more training on me. I shouldn't have been surprised the wolves in my life thought putting my head down and exhausting my body would take my mind off it. Stella at least brought cookies, which helped me swallow her positive attitude and lists. She came up with a new title for them every time, things like *Other Good Matches* or *Get to Know Better*. And Charlie, my best friend from Chicago, insisted that the first step to any successful breakup was getting every inch of your hair that had grown while you were together cut off.

I hadn't cut my hair since moving to Shady and it fell to my elbow. So one Friday, when I was feeling particularly miserable about the whole situation, I walked into the salon and waited until they could squeeze me in. Then asked them to take off more than a foot of it.

Riah was sitting on my front porch when I got home. He stood to meet me as I headed up the walk.

"You got your hair cut," he said with a bit of surprise.

"I just sent you a picture from the salon."

"But you cut it, cut it."

"All of Christian." It rested along my collarbone now. "Nearly two years' worth."

He smirked. "I like it."

"The haircut?"

"Definitely." His smirk had faded to one of his cuter smiles. "But mostly you cutting all of Christian off."

I shoved him playfully and we headed inside the house. "You'll have to text Charlie that you like her methods."

"I will." He cleared his throat and when I turned to raise an eyebrow at him, he wiped a strange expression off his face. "So, you want to run?"

I dropped my backpack on the floor in the little hall, then my winter coat on top of it. "It's freezing."

He shrugged. "Isn't it usually?"

I didn't love running, but I wasn't going to turn down time with him, especially if it was time Kiara wasn't with us. Even so, I made a face at the idea, then launched myself up the stairs as if we'd called a race. He caught up, and I tried to shove him out of the way so I could reach my bedroom first, but he was too sturdy and we barreled into it at the same time, nearly getting stuck. We burst into my room laughing.

He slumped onto my desk chair. "How terrible is it of me to break up with Kiara before the Valentine's dance?"

"Pretty terrible. Why do you want to break up with her?"

"Besides the obvious?"

"What's the obvious?"

He studied my eyes, as if I should know what he was talking about, but I honestly didn't. "Never mind."

Now I studied him, for answers he wasn't giving me, but talking about Kiara had always been a little awkward.

"We doing this or not?"

I grabbed for joggers, a hoodie, and fleece, then changed in my bathroom. We stretched in my living room, then jogged in place to warm up our muscles, not that it seemed to help much once we hit the sidewalk. The cold was bracing.

"Kiara keeps telling me she loves me," he said.

"That's why you want to break up with her?"

"Yeah."

"Because you don't love her." Thank goodness. She was kind of a slug. And by that, I meant she'd suctioned herself to him and slugged all over him. It made me roll my eyes on a regular basis.

"How'd you know you were in love with Christian?"

"I don't want to think about it."

"You can't expect to date him for two years and then get over him in a month."

The hair felt better, like relief, but it also felt empty. Like I was missing something I'd gotten really used to, something I was really comfortable with. Something I reached for without thinking about it. "But I *want* to be over him."

"And I want Kiara to stop loving me."

So she tells you she loves you, and what do you say back?

"Nice things I like about her."

I stopped running to laugh. He jogged back to me and grabbed my arm to keep me moving.

"I can only keep that up for so long," he admitted. "There are only so many things I like about her. It's awkward and I just want it to be over."

It would be cruel to break up with her before the dance. She bought you a tie that matches her dress, remember?

"I should have broken up with her right then. It's *orange*." Orange was Riah's least favorite color. He said there were very few pleasing shades of orange.

As we jogged past the high school, he picked up our pace a bit.

Maybe I didn't love Christian, I admitted.

He looked over at me in surprise.

He was so sure about us. I guess to some extent I went along with it. With his feelings.

Riah grunted. "I hope that's all you went along with."

I shoved him. It was like shoving a wall. You'd think I could catch him a little off balance while running, but no.

When we reached the main Shady intersection, we slowed to a stop. I folded over to put my hands on my knees while Riah strolled unaffected to the curb. I was warm enough from the running, but the air still bit at me. Fresh though. I took great big breaths of fresh air and appreciated every bit of them. "Have you asked Ethan and Stella their theories on love?"

"I know their theories on love," he grumbled. "They wouldn't shut up about it when they first got together."

I snorted. They were pretty gross as it was, I couldn't imagine how bad they might have been at the start, when Riah had been the third wheel.

"Have I ever told you how grateful I am that you showed up?" he asked.

The light turned and we crossed the street, heading in the direction of the movie theater. Straight would have brought us past the grocery store and Parrino's, toward the beach. Right went to Al's and the blood bank, then out of town.

"If you hadn't," he said, "I probably would have ended up hanging out with my sisters the rest of my life."

"Your sisters are pretty awesome."

"Maybe, but they're my sisters."

We started running again. "What do your sisters think about love?"

"Maribel thinks if it's the real thing, you just know. You don't doubt it. And Ava says it makes you desperate. That it *consumes* you."

I'd felt consumed with Christian in the beginning. But it couldn't have been love. It was too early. And then, when it might have been love, I was only desperate for him to stop being jealous. *Sometimes I'm desperate for chocolate.*

"Ethan and Stella say there's a tug. An invisible thread that keeps showing up and tugging you back."

I side-eyed him. "You really have made your rounds on this. How long has she been telling you she loves you?"

"It's not the first time I've thought about it."

Who was the first time you thought about it?

"You mean when?"

No, I mean who.

"I tend to believe Ethan and Stella. Ava's never had a relationship that lasted longer than a month, and Maribel makes it seem too simple."

Riah! Tell me who.

He glanced over at me. I couldn't run very well while looking at him, but he didn't seem to have any problems. After a few footfalls, he finally answered. "Aster."

That's baloney. That was, like, two weeks, and it was seventh grade.

"Three," Riah corrected, like he might actually be serious, before picking up his pace. I gave him the few feet between us without trying to keep up—I was too tired for that. We ran in silence past the movie theater and the fields until the road narrowed into a little dirt lane that led out to my grandparents' and Aster's.

There were maybe a dozen properties out here that had been sectioned off from Shady's original farm. You couldn't see any houses or old barns from the main road, only country lanes and long, skinny driveways. The forest that insulated Shady Woods spread across the horizon ahead of us, circling behind Riah's neighborhood to the left and around the lake to our right.

Even though I knew that, it felt like the middle of nowhere. I checked for my phone in my pocket, not even thinking about the Sentinel until we closed in on the tree line and I spotted them patrolling. Nehemiah's bashed in face came to mind, and I slipped my phone out of my pocket to unlock it, my thumb hovering over Aster's number. She always answered, she lived the closest, and she was a wolf. Between her and Riah, we could take two rogue Sentinels.

But it was just my brother and Clara.

I slowed, bending over to catch my breath, until Justin charged at me, jerking me up to look at him. "What are you doing out here?"

"Running." I yanked myself from his grip. "Geez."

Pulling his phone from his pocket, he dialed a number and stalked back over to Clara. She put a hand on his arm to soothe him and said something to Riah. I forced my tired legs to move so I could hear what they were saying.

"I need you to come get them," Justin said into the phone.

"We can walk back," I argued.

"Yeah, I'll keep them until you get here, thanks." He hung up. "Mom's coming."

"What is wrong with you?"

Justin crossed his arms but didn't say anything. Clara fiddled with the end of her long braid. "There's been a lot of wild activity on the edges of town."

"What kind of wild activity?" Riah asked.

"They just"—Clara shrugged—"roam it."

"They're hunting."

"They're hunting in town?" Riah asked.

"No." Clara set her chin on Justin's shoulder and kissed his cheek. "They leave to hunt."

"I don't get the problem," I said.

"I don't want you to get the problem," my brother snapped. "I want you to stay away from the edge of town. You think just because you're with Riah, you can go anywhere and do anything, but having a wolf on hand doesn't mean you're invincible."

"I feel oddly both complimented and insulted." Riah said, glancing my way while feeling up his biceps. "You must brag an awful lot about me. Think I'm invincible?"

I rolled my eyes.

"Grace, I'm serious." My brother had never begged me like this before. "Don't be out alone. Don't wander too far. Don't get lost."

"I'm not a stray, Justin. I'm not alone. And how could I possibly get lost in this tiny town? How 'bout you do your job?"

"This is me doing my job."

"No, this is you being a stupid brother. You're not telling Riah to take care of himself."

"Riah isn't at risk."

My heartbeat pounded in my ears. I wasn't sure if it was still trying to calm down after the run or if it was angry about things always coming back to this.

The wild vampires needed blood, but wolf and siren wouldn't do. We—the dendrites—were the weakest link. It was perfect timing for Charlie's daily text to ping into my phone, which she'd started the day Christian and I broke up.

I love you. You're perfect.

This was the first time it didn't manage to get a smile out of me. Because in Shady Woods, being perfect wasn't enough. In Shady Woods, you had to be stronger and tougher than perfect.

You had to be invincible.

Chapter Five

I'll Take One of Each

I didn't appreciate an audience while training, and I appreciated it even less when it included Kiara, particularly on the first afternoon I was training with a vampire.

I crossed my arms and faced Aster. "When I texted you that I needed to start sparring with a vampire, I meant Ethan."

Ethan glanced up from where he was nuzzling Stella's neck. Stella was working on a new list this morning, titled *Next Up*.

"Jeremy has more skills," Aster said, winding her curly hair up into a messy bun. "Sorry, Ethan."

Jeremy puffed out his slender chest. "I come from a long line of badasses."

I gave him a look. A long line of creepers was more like it. His dad ran the truck stop, had been the only gatekeeper of Shady before the Sentinel was created, and with his axe collection and the general schtick he used to run people off, he'd always come across as creepy to me, not dangerous. Granted, I'd only ever seen him when I'd been more strictly accustomed to normal. I tilted my head, curious if I'd get a totally different impression now.

"I can't exactly beat you yet," I said to Aster, not sure I was ready for Jeremy to lay into me. Ethan would definitely be nicer.

"You could if everything went your way, and that's probably as good as you'll get. You need to learn to fight speed now, not just strength."

Jeremy winked. "I'm all speed."

"Okay, so listen." Aster stood between us, futzing with the drawstrings on my sweatshirt and tucking my hair back into my ponytail as if she were my mother. "Jeremy's arms are longer than yours. Remember that, if you think you're within striking distance, he is too." This wasn't the case with her. "He's faster and longer. What you need to remember is that he is not necessarily stronger."

Jeremy crossed his arms. "I heard that."

"So when you think there's no hope, use your strength. Pummel him."

I frowned. "This isn't my first fight, Aster. I doubt I'll feel hopeless."

Her eyebrow quirked. "Maybe you should watch us first."

I rolled my eyes and gently pushed her aside. "You can't always watch how someone fights before you have to fight them."

Her brow furrowed and she stepped back a few feet. "Don't let him hold you at arm's length. You won't be able to reach him then."

She'd always urged me to stay out of reach before. The closer to a wolf, the harder they could land a punch.

"And remember your footwork." The footwork we'd worked on was to keep distance until I saw an opening. But she'd just told me to stay close to him. I suppose I'd still need to find an—

That quick, Jeremy was behind me, lips on my neck. "Gotcha."

With a shiver, I shoved him away. At least he'd kept his fangs in check. "We hadn't started, Jer."

He winked at me. "The start of a fight is not always going to be up to you."

"Do not put Gabe on there," Riah said, reading Stella's list from where he stood behind her, Kiara curled around his arm.

"Why not?"

"Wolves are too hairy for her."

I gave him a look and he smirked at me.

"I'll take a Gabe," Aster said.

Jeremy glanced over at them and I took the opportunity to sucker-punch him in the face.

"Ow!" he cried, but with a grin, like he was impressed.

I shrugged. "You don't always know when it's coming."

He laughed as his skin knit itself back together.

"Oh, that's handy," Aster said. She and I had given each other more than a few cuts and bruises over the last year.

"Yes." I grinned at him. "Why didn't we think of this sooner?"

"Also." Aster stepped forward, finger up between us before turning to me. "I clearly failed to mention that a vampire isn't going to try to get their hands on you. They're going to try to get their fangs in you, from behind."

A wolf did try to get their hands on you. They liked to rip open their meat before they ate it, and this translated to how they fought as well, or so Aster told me.

"If he does get behind you, you lean forward and kick back to give yourself the space to turn around. Instead of drilling the elbows, punches, and nut shots, I want you to start drilling kicks, okay?"

Since Jeremy was currently in front of me, I leaned back and kicked forward, aiming high for Jeremy's hip. He shoved Aster out of the way, knocked my other foot out from under me, caught me around the waist, and twisted us so that when we hit the ground, he was beneath me. Then, just as vampire-fast, he flipped us over and pressed his lips to my neck.

I sighed. It was like starting all over. Which shouldn't surprise me, because that was how it went in skills too. Starting a new thing was always hard, no matter how powerful I'd felt with the material that came before it.

"This is going to be loads of fun," Jeremy said, rolling off me, while Aster held her hand out to help me up.

"Don't put Johnny on there," Ethan said.

Stella rolled her eyes to him. "Why not?"

"Because of how he talks in the locker room," Riah answered.

Aster plopped down in the seat next to Stella. "I'll take a Johnny."

"Aren't you cold?" I asked them. All of them. "Don't you want to go inside?"

Nearly in unison, they looked up at the sun. It had melted out the snow, but the ground was still hard enough that it wasn't wet and muddy, and the temp today was hovering in the forties. After the kind of winter we'd had, I guess I couldn't blame them for jumping at an excuse to spend some time outside.

"I don't mind an audience," Jeremy said.

"We know you don't," I muttered.

"Oh!" Aster perked up. "Sending emotion is more disorienting to a vampire than a wolf. You could try that again. They aren't used to emotion the way we are."

"You can try anything on me," Jeremy offered. "Shock me even. Next time my mouth is on your neck, use that fear to channel your telelectrical output."

"It might help if I was actually scared of you." Reality was, though, I hadn't had any luck yet in class. It was not something I could hope for or count on.

Jeremy twitched, and I turned, anticipating that he was going to try to get around me again. Vampires didn't move faster than human sight, but trying to stay in front of him did make me a little dizzy. I managed long enough to be nearly out of breath, got one good kick in, and then suddenly he was behind me, this time with his arm around my waist, his fangs clicking down to rest on my neck.

I froze. I wasn't afraid of him. I trusted him. Still, it was terrifying. What if he slipped?

"Use it," he whispered.

But I couldn't move. Couldn't risk him accidentally pricking my skin.

"I have good bite inhibition, Grace. Use the fear."

I went to shake my head, then thought better of it and squeezed my eyes tight. My breathing was heavy and his was heavy—was his heavy because he was so close to fresh blood? I screamed in both our heads, which had him clenching my waist tighter to him, but instead of retracting his fangs or pushing me away like I thought he might, he clenched my waist tighter against him.

"Jeremy," I whimpered, opening my eyes on Riah's narrowed gaze.

"Shock me," he demanded.

I tried. I tried to focus enough to channel anything at all into my fingers but came up with nothing. He held me for a long time, until my body surrendered, resting against him, until he'd retracted the fangs and left one single long kiss pressed against my skin, while slowly trailing his hand back along my waist to release me.

Aster raised an eyebrow. Stella scribbled another name on her list.

"No," Riah said, resolutely.

Kiara tugged at him. When it didn't pull his gaze from mine, she said, "Riah, tell them about the musician's gala."

"What about the musician's gala?" Stella asked, jotting a few more names down.

"Ooh." Aster nodded. "I'll take one of each of those as well."

Riah watched me until Jeremy was many feet away, then watched Jeremy. Kiara nudged him again.

"Remember the film awards?" she asked us. "Same thing happened with the musician's gala last weekend." She waited for Riah to continue, but he seemed slightly frozen in place. "One blamed meningitis and someone else malaria, of all things. Malaria, in America." Kiara clicked her tongue. "Another said they had a brain abscess. I mean, what are the odds?"

"That second siren movie better still come out on time or I will seriously throw a fit." Stella twisted back to study Riah, then scribbled another name in her notebook. Aster snickered. Ethan squinted at it, his gaze skipping over me and Riah and Kiara, then took the notebook from her and closed the cover.

"Have you ever read the symptoms of meningitis, malaria, and brain abscesses?" Kiara shook Riah's arm. "Tell them."

I raised an eyebrow, wondering if this was one of the things he liked about her, that she entertained his conspiracy theories.

"Headaches, fever, disorientation, and dizziness, for starters."

"Remind you of anything else?" Kiara asked. "Not to mention, have you seen any pictures of Jenny Jones lately? She's taller."

"Wait." My attention focused. "You think they're vampires now?"

Kiara nodded for him. "Tell them about the full moon vacations."

"The celebrities who missed the film awards are saying that the full moon messes with their creativity."

"The full moon messes with everything," Aster agreed.

Jeremy cleared his throat. "I feel like I can only attack you so many times while you're completely distracted."

I frowned at him, at how he was studying me.

"Not that I mind how it ends up."

Crossing my arms, I studied him right back. He wanted to make me feel like meat, well, I could do the same thing. To be honest, he wasn't hard to look at, the vampire angles working for him in a way they didn't for everyone, and his olive-toned skin contrasting in the best way with the green of his eyes. If you looked for too long, he might take your breath away a little bit, which was why every girl at school had fallen for him at one time or another, and why I'd said yes to him showing me around town when I first got here.

Most of all, though, his lips. Not the reputation that preceded them, but how they were formed into a natural pout, and how they were not angular at all.

I rolled my eyes at him, and myself—at how a simple name on a piece of paper could put an idea in your head— then dropped into ready stance once again.

Chapter Six

It's a Small Town

On the way to physics the next day, I ran into Nehemiah. He was coming from the opposite direction. Or maybe he'd just been standing there in the middle of the hall, seeing as how the sea of students spun around him like he was a rock in the middle of whitewater.

"Grace," he said as I approached.

"Nehemiah." I nodded and tried to squeeze around him, but he stepped in front of me. His face was back to normal, aside from the scruff that he'd let grow.

"If we're going out tonight, you should call me Miah."

"Oh." What?

"Great. I'll meet you in the lot. I think we're parked pretty close to each other. I'll drive."

"I'm, um... I'm giving blood after school."

"Perfect. I'll pick you up from there. Figured we'd leave town anyway."

"I'm sorry, but, I just broke up with my boyfriend. Probably not a good idea."

"I know. The whole school was abuzz. Anyway, it's a great idea."

I opened my mouth, but before I could make it clear that I wasn't going anywhere with him, he was gone.

"He was not on my list," Stella said, sliding up next to me. She rummaged through the pile of notebooks in her arms. "Should I add him to my list?"

Jeremy appeared on my other side and the three of us headed into class. "Are we actually dating again?"

"No."

"We should be." Stella set her pile of notebooks on her desk. They tumbled like an avalanche. "But Nehemiah wasn't on my list."

Jeremy caught one that was about to spill to the floor. "Pretty sure Nehemiah wouldn't make the cut. Did anyone actually make the cut yesterday?"

Stella winked at him. "Only the ones Riah didn't see."

"Who would you put on *my* list?" he asked her.

"Aster and Kevin and every other person you've already dated."

"Kevin?" I echoed.

"Yes, Kevin. Better to recycle Jeremy than horrify anyone new."

He gave her a look. "If by horrify, you mean enlighten."

"I'm an ex of his, too," I pointed out. "Sort of."

Stella stared at me. She was right, I shouldn't have mentioned it. We didn't need to repeat the Worst First Date in History. I hadn't said it because I wanted him on the list, anyway.

I glanced at Jeremy. "You and Aster, you and Kevin, and then Kevin and Aster?"

He shrugged. "It's a small town."

The bell rang and Mr. Reinard clapped his hands. "I'd like to do something different today," he said, once we'd all quieted. "I'd like to have a class discussion about Shady's newest arrivals."

The class looked around, as if we had a new student.

"I'm talking about the wilds who've joined us. Surely you've ran into one or two on the street. They're a bit restless, of course, which I'd say is pretty normal."

"I'd say they're twitchy," muttered someone in the back row.

"Precisely why I think we should discuss them. This town was built on tenets that would have us welcoming the wilds with open arms, enfolding them into our lifestyle, helping them adjust."

Nora raised her hand from the front row. Mr. Reinard nodded at her. "I welcomed one," she said, "and they immediately told me we should live like this everywhere. Living out loud, they called it. *That* is not the point of Shady."

Reinard crossed his arms, which he often did when he was weighing how exactly to handle a student, but Nora was the last person a teacher would need to handle. She was already slinking back, wilting under his gaze.

"Who else thinks we're not worthy of living out loud?" he finally asked, which caused the room to go completely silent. A delicately phrased question. Some people looked around, as if double checking that he'd actually went there.

"What kind of question is that?" a senior countered.

"Pick a side," Mr. Reinard said, walking down the center aisle. "Those who feel like arguing for traditional Shady on the left, and those who feel like arguing for living out loud on the right. Let's all assume you're choosing a side for argument's sake, not because you believe in it whole-heartedly, and perhaps we can foster a bit of understanding."

We were already sitting on the left, so Stella and I didn't move, but Jeremy stood up. He didn't go anywhere, but he stood up.

I glared at him.

"What?" he mouthed, throwing up his hands like I should know both sides held possibility, then dragged his desk to the middle of the aisle. We were in the back, so it almost looked like he was planning to referee.

After the shuffling was over, Mr. Reinard asked who'd like to start. "One of the seniors, I think. Have any of you given thought to what you want to do after high school? How you want to live?"

"We're not expected to give that any thought," a senior from our side said. "We stay here. We do this."

A wolf across the room raised his hand. "Maybe that's the problem. Maybe we should be able to go out in the world without having to hide in sewers. Imagine how demoralizing, when we're at the top of the food chain."

"You don't think normals, once they realized they were prey, would try to eradicate us?" a siren on our side stood. "It's not worth death to me. Is it worth death to you?"

The wolf shrugged. "If we turned all the normals, everyone would be on the same playing field. No eradication necessary."

"No eradication necessary?" I cried. "That would be eradicating humans!"

"Okay, but"—Jeremy out his hands up—"if we turned all the normals, who would we drink from?"

"Dendrites, obviously."

"And just like that"—someone behind me snapped their fingers—"dendrites end up the second-class citizens."

A vampire on the side that was starting to sound quite elitist rolled his eyes. "You already provide your blood. What difference would it make, hiding here or living freely out there?"

"We don't do it because we like it," the same voice snapped. "We do it because it's the right thing to do. Besides, there aren't enough of us."

"There definitely wouldn't be if you turned all the humans into vampires," one of us agreed.

"Exactly. It's not realistic."

I glanced around and noted that the line was mostly—not entirely, but mostly—divided with dendrites and sirens on the traditional Shady side, and vampires and wolves on the elitist side.

"Has everyone forgot there are more of them than us?" Nora asked. "Eradication would feel like a dream if we ended up on a table, dissected."

"We do have a long and sordid history with humans," muttered a siren next to her.

"It would be a disaster," she agreed.

"So, humans either kill us, dissect us, or we turn them all into wolves and vampires," a siren to my left muttered. "Then, the vampires suck all the dendrite blood until there's none left. Meaning it's either hide like we're doing now, or best case, end up a society of wolves and sirens."

"Perfect," a beefy, elitist wolf grinned. "We'll take the land and you can go back to the water."

"The only foreseeable end to an elitist society is a hunter/prey situation, or slavery," said the only African American in our class. Northern Wisconsin was pretty white. Nora's mom was Japanese, Aster's dad was Native American, Jeremy had a thread of Middle Eastern far back in his lineage, and that was about it. "Haven't we learned anything as a people, to not go back there?"

The elitist wolf who'd started the conversation stood to prop himself on his desk with his knuckles. "There's nothing in our collective abnormal histories that tells of anything like slavery."

"We're not better than humans just because we didn't own slaves," I argued. "The elitist mentality is exactly what created slavery in the first place. And if you don't think abnormals have the same capacity for darkness, you're crazy."

"There has to be a way to compromise," Jeremy said. "A way for vampire blood and siren tears to help the world as a whole, to help the humans rise with us."

"That's not elitist, if they're rising with us." And pretty much the entire elitist side of the room turned on him.

"They're a step above animals."

"They're sacs of blood."

"They're people, just like us." My voice was strong and clear and cut through their murmurings. Jeremy looked at me helplessly, and Stella shot me a grateful, calming bit of charm. I stood up this time. "I think before anyone decides where humans fall on the food chain, they should get to know a few of them. We might be able to do things that they can't, but the great discoveries of this world are not exclusive to dendrites. And our history is not less full of wars and power-hungry men than theirs is."

"In order to get to know them"—beefy elitist smirked—"we'd have to live out loud."

Jeremy scooched his desk back to its original position, on the traditional Shady side. It caught everyone's attention. As if in explanation, he said, "We should be able to help each other, without killing or using each other."

"Survival of the fittest, that's their philosophy, isn't it? We're the fittest."

I was actually shaking when the bell rang. Stella wrapped me in a soft blanket of charm and I sank into it, hardly realizing that Jeremy was walking me to my locker.

"Remember when you called me an elitist on our first date?" he asked.

I nodded.

"That's what I was thinking about when I took their side."

"Guess you're really your own breed."

An absent-minded half smile crossed his face. "Which is what?"

I shrugged as we reached my locker. "Whatever term you want to coin for someone who wants to live in the open and help everyone rise together."

"That didn't sound naive?"

I squinted at him a little. "I didn't know Jeremy Holmes ever second-guessed himself."

He leaned a thin shoulder against the lockers. Man, he was tall. I'd grown a bit but still barely reached his chin. "Just where you're concerned."

With a snort, I rolled my eyes. He was such a player.

"I'm serious!" He looked offended. "I don't have the same effect on you that I do on everyone else."

With a short laugh, I shoved my books in my locker. Freshman year, when I'd first arrived in Shady, before Christian and I ever happened, Jeremy and I had gone out once. It was terrible. So terrible that when he tried to kiss me, I was so surprised I spit him away.

"I know it's short notice, Grace, but if you're really dating again, I'd like to take you to the dance."

"Like, as friends?"

"Sure."

I studied his face and considered this. If I said no, it would be me, Stella and Ethan, Riah and Kiara, and Aster and Christian. Yeah. Christian had asked Aster as friends, so I could go with Jeremy as friends. Right?

"Okay, sure."

"Great."

Riah shook his head from his locker after Jeremy was out of earshot. "Not him again."

"Not *again*. Didn't you hear? We're going as friends."

He raised an eyebrow at me.

"Jeremy can have friends, Riah."

"Is this your way of getting back at Christian?"

I frowned and bit my tongue to keep from protesting. Sometimes, Riah knew me better than I knew myself. Or rather, could smell me better than I knew myself. So I took a minute. Could that have been any part of my motivation? I mean, if I'd been aiming for a date who would get back at Christian, I could have done much better. Riah, for example. But that's not what I wanted, was it? So why did it feel sort of satisfying somewhere deep inside?

Hurting Christian wouldn't change anything. It wouldn't make us even and it wouldn't make it okay.

Regardless, when I walked into skills, I felt like he should hear it from me.

I started with an easy, *Aster said you two were going to the dance together. Asked if you could come with us.*

She said you were okay with it.

It seemed cruel to tell him I didn't really want him there, almost as cruel as him somehow managing to insert himself into my evening. He could have asked any other girl at the school. Aster said he wasn't ready to date, though, and since he clearly had a difficult time being alone... Ugh, I was thinking way too much about this.

He settled his right hand on my knee, and I settled my right hand on his. Our free hands were on our own knee, so if we managed to transfer any electricity from our fingers, we'd know as soon as our partner.

So far, as a class, no one had.

I'm bringing Jeremy then.

Christian's focus shot up to my face. "What?"

Mr. Turner clucked. "Ms. James and Mr. Riley, you are not to be speaking right now. Focus on the output."

"Of course," I said, but my voice hitched on the *course,* because, "Ow!" Not that it actually hurt; it was more of a surprise than anything.

In a flurry, the entire class was around us, silent and waiting.

Christian's eyes were wide as he held my gaze. "I'm sorry?"

I snorted. *Don't be. It didn't hurt.*

Eyes on mine, he shocked me again, then turned his fingers over so everyone could see the blue haze as it dissipated.

We're just going as friends, if that's what this is about.

Another zap.

"He's getting stronger each time." Not that they couldn't all see it. The sparks were brighter and fatter and longer and moved more with a mind of their own.

"Impressive, Mr. Riley. I'd imagined it would be another week before anyone managed this."

Shock, shock, shock.

The class started mumbling and moved back to their seats newly motivated.

I, on the other hand, sat there like a sitting duck, caught somewhere between impressed and angry that he was taking it out on me, after what *he'd* done. I should be able to shock him, too. I should've been able to shock him first. But I couldn't.

Even now, I couldn't. Clearly his anger was greater than whatever was left of mine, and I told myself that was good. That was better. That meant I didn't care enough to be angry.

It meant I was over him. And I smiled.

Chapter Seven

Pint or Live Feed

The blood bank had all the makings of an actual bank—lobby, drive thru, vault, tellers, offices. Though, the offices were set up to take blood, not discuss financial accounts.

I stepped up to the counter and waited for a teller to finish with someone at the window. Another was coming out of the vault and smiled at me. She headed over first.

"Deposit or withdrawal?"

"Deposit. I have an appointment for 4:10. James, Grace."

She scanned the computer in front of her, squinting until she found me. "Pint or live feed?"

I blinked at her. This was a new question. "What?"

"Vampires drink a little more quickly, so that saves some time, if you're in a hurry. Would you like me to explain the process?"

I held the counter to steady myself. "The process of a live feed?"

She nodded, seemingly unaffected by this turn of events.

"Since when have you offered that?"

"Last week. We'd talked about it since the wolves started hunting in Shady, but having some wilds around pushed us to actually try it." She shrugged. "It's been well received."

How many wilds were actually here, that they'd make this massive change in how they distributed the town's blood supply? Or were enough Shady vampires angling for this that the wilds only offered an excuse?

Swallowing hard, I glanced behind me at the offices. There were four, each with one nice-sized window you could see out of but not into.

"If you're not sure," the woman in front of me said, "you can watch before you decide."

I shook my head. "Pint, please. Traditional."

She smiled. "Would you like me to make that the default in your account?"

"Yes."

"Great. Take a seat. They'll be out for you in a moment."

As I slumped down in one of the chairs lined up outside the offices, Violet Parrino walked in. She wore loose-fitting jeans and a men's suit jacket. Mr. Parrino's clothing, I assumed, given this outfit matched the length of her.

She went up to the counter, gave them her name, said she was here for a live feed, and was told to take a seat as well. It did not seem like the first time she'd done this. She landed a few chairs over from me, and I tried not to react to the fact that had I offered myself up, she would be the one drinking from an open cut on my body. On top of the obvious horror of it, it occurred to me that it might feel a bit intimate, such an exchange.

"How long do you usually have to wait?" I blurted out.

She brushed her curly hair out of her face as she noticed me. "Oh. Grace, right?"

I nodded.

Sliding over a seat, she smiled. "If none of the next few appointments choose to be a live donation, then one of the staff will sit for me."

With a hard swallow, I averted my gaze and told myself not to ask for specifics. I did not want to know. I had to repeat that last bit a few times, though, because I kind of did want to know. But I didn't.

Violet slid over another seat, next to me now, and held out her phone. "I have pictures of Ethan and Riah when they were little. Want to see?"

I checked the screen out of the corner of my eye, waiting for my brain to make the full switch from blood-sucking wild to soft mother figure. The lock screen on her phone did it pretty quickly, Ethan and Eric sitting on the stoop with ice cream cones dripping down their hands.

Dark red ice cream, but still.

"*Yes*," I replied emphatically. "Of course I want to see."

It was their four-digit street address she typed in to unlock her phone, and it opened onto her social media app, full of celebrities and influencers. The woman was shifting shape in front of me, wild heartless vampire to mother hooked on Hollywood gossip.

I watched her face, her soft smile as she closed out of the app and pulled up pictures of the boys when they were little. She'd been living in the shadows, carrying around pictures of her boys and following celebrity lives. But then I was quickly overcome with cute baby cheeks, that pout of Riah's I still got glimpses of sometimes, and Ethan's crossed-arm, I'm-a-vampire, you-can't-ruffle-me stance that he'd apparently perfected when he was four. She asked if I wanted her to send them to me—*yes*—so I gave her my number and we laughed over the best ones, the ones she then pinged to my phone, until they called my name.

The technician got me stuck and situated, and while my blood drained into the bag, I sent the baby pictures to our group chat so Stella and Aster could coo over them with me.

When I came out of the room after giving blood, Violet and another woman were being led into the room next to me. Though the baby pictures and mom talk had soothed me for a bit, this reality brought me full circle back to agitated.

That's not really any excuse as to why I got in Nehemiah's car when I saw him waiting for me like he said he'd be, but I suddenly needed to get out of town, away from all this. I didn't care that it was discouraged, I only cared that there was now a live feed at the blood bank.

I slid into his passenger seat without a word and stared out his windshield at the brown brick of the blood bank.

It was hard to swallow. It felt more momentous somehow than the town council election had.

"You all right?" he asked.

I blinked.

"Grace?"

"They do live feeds now."

"Yeah, Preston told me. Creepy as—"

"Where do you go when you leave town?" I interrupted. "Where are we going?"

He shrugged. "There's a lot of cute places in Marinette. Well, more cute places when the weather is nice, but we could go to the diner there, or a movie."

Marinette was north. I'd never been further north than Shady. I nodded and tried to swallow my horror. If he did nothing else for me than allowed me to forget about the live feeds for a little bit, allowed me to pretend once again that life was normal, I'd be grateful.

As he pulled past Silver Subs, the Sentinel stationed there were standing off the road with a handful of vampires. A couple of them began to walk into the street when Nehemiah didn't turn into the last driveway, but he sped past them before they could stop us. He threw up a little wave.

"That why they beat you up?" I asked.

"Because I didn't stop to explain myself on the way out? No."

"Maybe if you had, they wouldn't have been as upset when you came back in."

He glanced over at me. "That's cute, Grace." Then he turned the music up and started singing at the top of his lungs. He had a decent voice—nothing like Christian's, but decent— and whether he meant it as some sort of therapeutic release or not, that's how it felt, so I joined him.

I never would have sung along with Christian. His voice was meant to be heard and savored. Plus, I would have sounded like total crap singing with him. And I could hold a tune just fine.

By the time we reached the diner in Marinette, I was grinning. Nehemiah turned off the car, and in the silence, my smile faded. But I felt a lot better. "Thank you."

"You're welcome."

"Did you do that for me?" I asked as we walked across the parking lot. "Or because it's just something you do?"

"You smelled like you needed to get some frustration out."

Ah. Right. Wolf. "I did need to get some frustration out," I admitted.

"Singing with someone is a lot less weird than screaming with them."

I laughed. "You're an expert?"

"In getting frustration out?" His gaze slid sideways to me. "Yeah."

And there was that little bit of creepy I'd gotten in the grocery store when Charlie was here freshman year. Thankful for the lights in the diner, I reminded myself that Nehemiah was harmless. He was. I truly believed that. There was much worse in Chicago. Hell, there was much worse back in Shady.

Things were a little awkward while we looked at the menu and ordered our food, awkward enough that I realized this was a date I was on. He asked about my life growing up, about living human and what I missed about the city, besides the people. I ended up going on and on about Chicago in a way I hadn't thought of in years. I did love the city. The pulse. The noise and the excitement of all those lives intersecting. Things *happened* in a city.

"Did you know any werewolves in Chicago?" Nehemiah asked, once our food arrived. He'd ordered a Reuben with extra sauerkraut, which I hoped meant I wouldn't need to deflect a kiss in my future.

"As far as I know, everyone in Chicago is normal." This couldn't actually be true, of course. Now that I knew about wilds and how they lived, I knew that the bigger the city—the more crime—the easier to hide.

"But it must be easy to blend in."

"Not exactly." I placed my napkin on my lap and really looked at him, so he'd hopefully hear me. "You'd have to give up hope of anyone truly being able to understand you. You'd have to get used to feeling caged. You might think you feel caged in Shady, but so many little things about who you are..." I shook my head. "You can't understand what you have to hide until you're trying to hide it all at once." I hadn't even understood it, until I'd lived long enough both ways. The trip last year when we met my old friends in Madison was stifling.

He pouted a little. "Besides the night of the full moon, what would be a problem?"

"You'd have to hide your strength and act like you didn't know what everyone was feeling all the time. Sure, normals eat raw meat, but only sometimes, and as a delicacy."

"Maybe I'll open a restaurant. Make it cool."

I offered him a sad smile. I wished it were that easy; I wanted both worlds myself. But the longer I was here, the more I wasn't sure that was possible. "Maybe there's a way to meet up with other abnormals in the city. Probably, I guess. I don't know. But then you have kids and they screw up and you end up back here."

He pushed his plate aside. "I don't want kids."

"What do you want?"

"I want to live normal."

"You'd have to hide every cool thing about you," I pointed out.

He grinned. "You think I'm cool?"

I gave him a look. "That's not what I meant."

"I'd have to hide every abnormal thing about me, but I'd be able to see the world."

"Wilds see the world." Or so I imagined.

"I'm too soft to be a wild after growing up in Shady. In a house, with a bed. And hot water."

"See? You'd miss it."

"I wouldn't miss the small minds."

I frowned. The minds in town did seem to be getting smaller. Or more complicated. Or more questionable. But— "It's safer there."

"Safe isn't all it's cracked up to be."

"Hiding huge parts of yourself isn't all it's cracked up to be."

"Hiding isn't cracked up to be anything. Why do you think the elitists won those council seats?"

My frown deepened and I opened my mouth to ask him if he considered himself an elitist, but he answered before I could get it out.

"No, I'm not behind the council or what they're doing. I'd be happy to hide, I'd just prefer to hide in the city. Think of the good I could do, walking the streets at night, saving people from being mugged or attacked or..." He grew uncomfortable under my gaze, which made me think 'raped' was the word he was having trouble getting out.

Here was the kid everyone thought was a problem—the epitome of rebellion in Shady Woods—and all he wanted was to be a hero. "That doesn't sound like hiding," I said.

"Humans can be strong, too. I'll just tell everyone I have a steroid problem."

I let out a short, surprised laugh, and a lazy smile grew on his face.

"Did you travel when you were normal?" he asked. "Or have you only seen Chicago?"

"We traveled."

He picked apart every day of every trip my family had ever taken before locking ourselves up in Shady Woods, then drove me by the frozen icicle lighthouse on the way home, asking if I wanted to stop and park there for a bit.

No, I did not. Particularly when there was another car and another couple steaming up the windows nearby.

On our way back to Shady, we sang at the top of our lungs again, only turning down the volume and slowing our speed after we rounded the truck stop and neared the edge of town. And only then because the street was blocked by four dark figures.

They were lined up in the center of the road like they'd been waiting for us, and they didn't move until Nehemiah pulled to a complete stop. The ones on either end walked to each of our windows, a third walked around to the back of the car, and the fourth stayed put. One on each side of us, so we couldn't pull forward or back out.

Nehemiah rolled down both of our windows simultaneously.

"License, please," they echoed.

I went to pull mine out, but Nehemiah held an arm across me like my mom used to when she had to make a hard stop. "You're supposed to keep the rats out. Not the citizens. Do we look like rats?"

"Let's not do this again."

"If you remember me, if you know I'm a citizen already, why bother with my license?"

"It's procedure."

"Yeah, you're so into *procedure*." This was when I remembered what Preston had said about his face, that the Sentinel didn't take kindly to Nehemiah's mouth. I reached over his arm for my wallet.

"Turn your car off, Nehemiah," the Sentinel near him repeated.

Settling an elbow out the open window, one hand still on the steering wheel, Nehemiah took his foot off the brake, letting his car roll ever so slowly forward. The Sentinel in front of us was many feet away. At no risk. I handed my license to the guy at my window, but instead of taking it, he yanked open the door and tugged me out of the car. Quick and easy. I landed on the asphalt with a huff.

The wolf in the path of Miah's headlights moved forward and planted both hands on his hood to stop it.

Miah had been yanked out of the car too, and punches were being thrown. I couldn't see much, but it looked like Miah was taking it. One more thing to report, like he'd said before. Did the police have any control over the Sentinel, though? The police might still be law in town, but the Sentinel, as best I could tell, reported to the council.

"I'm Justin James' sister," I told the guy standing over me. Reaching for my license, where it had fallen, I held it up for him. "I did not resist."

"You do look like him." He didn't take the license, but held out his own hand, like he was offering to help me up.

No, thank you very much. Getting up on my own, I held a sore wrist and stifled a groan for my tailbone. My palm stung too, the skin scraped up from catching myself.

Real nice.

As the sound of fists slowed from the other side of the car, I closed my eyes. There was nothing I could do. Miah could defend himself if he wanted to, far better than I could.

Not that it mattered. These guys might as well have been cops. That's the leeway I knew they'd been given. It made me think of the other day when Riah and I had run into Justin and Clara. He'd been so worried about what the wilds might do to me, but Violet was harmless compared to this. What my brother should be worried about was the Sentinel and what they were doing.

I slid back inside the car, shutting the door and closing my window. The woman with her hands on the hood stared at me.

"I need to get home!" I shouted at her, hoping it would jolt the Sentinel beating on Nehemiah to stop. Hoping the one on my side might relay that I was Justin's sister. Justin. One of them. Since clearly being a citizen of town wasn't enough.

"I'm about done, sugar," the vampire said, licking his lips. One more kick, a final oomph out of Nehemiah, and the four of them moved to form the same line they'd held as we'd approached, only behind us now.

When Miah didn't appear right away, I leaned over his seat to peer out at him. "Are you okay?"

He grinned. Or tried to grin. And pulled himself up. "I'm great. They're so stupid. They play right into my hands."

I sat, quietly digesting, while he drove the short block to the blood bank.

"What's your curfew?" he asked as he pulled in next to my car. It was a bit after 8:30 and I had to be home by 10.

"Nine," I lied.

He leaned over, and I moved out of the way.

"Too soon?" he asked, clearly not one bit unsettled about what had just occurred. But I was unsettled. My insides were shaky. I couldn't decide if it was rage or indignance or fear.

"Next time you take someone on a date out of town, don't ask for a fight coming back in."

"I can't control them, Grace."

"You can control yourself," I snapped, getting out of his car.

Once in my own, I stared out the windshield at the property that backed up to the blood bank. Nehemiah didn't leave right away, like he wanted to make sure my car would start, so I started it. When he'd finally gone, I called my brother.

"Hey, Squirrel." His normal greeting.

"The Sentinel just roughed me up."

"Where are you? You call Dad?"

"No, I'm fine. But they really laid into Nehemiah, and they didn't care that I saw it."

"Yeah."

"*Yeah?*" I headed to Stella's. "They didn't even care after they knew I was your sister!"

"Yeah." His tone was different on that one. Resigned.

"Justin! Is this why you were worried about me the other day? Is it the wilds, or was it that if we'd run into different Sentinel—not you and Clara—it might have gone down like this?"

He sighed into the phone. "Plenty of us would never act like that, even if it's expected."

"Expected?" I cried, taking a left toward the beach. "But you let the wilds in no problem!"

"The wilds are good at sneaking. It's what they do. Nehemiah isn't. No one likes how much he leaves town. You know it puts us at risk."

"So you'd beat the crap out of him, had it been you?"

"Wait." I could hear him shift the phone to his other ear. He did that a lot. "Did you leave town with Nehemiah?"

"Yes."

"Did you go on a *date* with Nehemiah?"

"No. We're just friends."

"Okay, but are you seeing him again?"

"No. Answer my question."

"What was your question again?"

Go already, lady! was dropped in my head, most likely from the guy behind me who punctuated each word with a beep. I blinked and realized I'd slowed to a complete stop in front of the park. Quickly, and with no apologies, I took my turn.

"Would you have beaten the crap out of Nehemiah, if it had been you on duty tonight?"

"Of course not."

"What if I wasn't in the car?"

"No. He's tried to goad me before. I don't take the bait."

"Does the Sentinel treat wilds like that too, or just town residents?"

"I told you, they know to sneak. And they usually come through the woods on foot. Who's going to be following them on foot? We're in the middle of nowhere."

"Samuel followed those Hand members through the woods on foot last year," I muttered, turning off my car. Stella noticed me, flipped on her porch light, and held open her front door.

My brother got distracted by Clara, something about ice cream and what show they should start.

"How many wilds are here?" I finally asked. "How many wilds are in town?"

"I don't know. We report them to the council as best we can. That's who keeps track."

With a sigh, I told him to go eat his ice cream and tell Clara I said hi. Then I hung up and got out of the car.

As I neared Stella, I held my palm up in the air. "Will you fix this for me?"

She narrowed her eyes. "Nehemiah do that?"

"No. Not directly." Sweeping past her to her kitchen, I hopped on the counter.

Holding my palm in her hand, she dripped tears ever so elegantly from her eyes to pool there. "Christian said he was pulling into the blood bank when you guys were pulling out. He texted me, asked what I knew about it."

I rolled my eyes.

She closed my palm on the little ocean she'd cried, and I shivered as it wiggled its way into my skin. "Are you hurt anywhere else?"

"Barely and not visibly. I just didn't want to bring this home to my parents."

She hopped up next to me, her strawberry-blonde hair nearly reaching the counter between us. "You don't want them to know what the Sentinel is doing?"

"I don't want them to know I left town." They wouldn't understand. Or they'd take it to mean I wanted to move back normal, which I most certainly did not.

I wiped Stella's silver tears off on my jeans and watched them evaporate into a fine dusty sheen. Tears threatened my own eyes, but I couldn't tell if they were for Christian or good friends or the Sentinel or what the wilds meant for Shady Woods.

Stella leaned into me and whispered, "Next time, stick to my list."

Chapter Eight

Dinner with a Vampire

"My mom will tell you everything you want to know if you try the blood pie," Ethan said, as we sat down in the cellar of his dad's restaurant to wait for his mom and her friends. "She's the one who put it on the menu in the first place."

"I'll do better than try it." I promised. "I ate an entire serving of the house marinara, remember?"

"And promptly threw up," Riah reminded.

"No." I raised a finger. "I threw up when I found out it was made of blood. That was mental. I have no mental barriers to blood any longer."

With a raised eyebrow, Ethan slid a shot glass over to me. It was part of the Parrino trio that they served in the cellar. Needless to say, they mostly sat vampires down here. "That's the feline," he said. "For contentment."

I pushed it back. "If only it would actually work on me."

Ethan's mom had wanted to make this dinner happen since she got here, and as soon as Ethan started warming to the idea, I jumped on it. After the live feeds and the way Justin talked about the wilds, I decided there was no better way to get a full picture than by going to the source.

This didn't mean I wasn't nervous, and I would have valued a little manufactured contentment.

Ethan had pushed together two tables to fit us all, and we were grouped on one side. He checked his phone. "They're late."

"They're wilds," Riah replied. "Of course they're late."

"Look at this picture of Jenny Jones." Stella handed Riah her phone. "Isn't she, like, twenty-five? You don't grow a foot at twenty-five."

"Not unless you've turned into a vampire," he muttered.

"Stop encouraging him," Ethan said to Stella.

"It's nearly impossible to tell how tall anyone is from a picture." I leaned into Riah to read the headline. A tabloid was reporting that she'd grown a foot in the last few months. They had set two pictures side by side as proof. "You think they're tall but they're tiny, and vice versa. It all depends who they're on screen with."

"It wouldn't be the stupidest way to come out," Stella said. "Everyone wants to be like the celebrities and influencers."

Riah handed her phone back. "If you wanted to out us and wanted the masses to follow…"

"Right? It's like pre-work. Get the famous people turned so when you blow out the secret, everyone will be clamoring to be like them, to be a part of it."

"Hell," Ethan muttered. "Turn a few influencers and they'd probably be happy to blow the secret out for you."

I sputtered mid-gulp of water. "If someone's turning them on purpose…" I took a moment to wrap my mind around this. "They're turning wolves too?"

The four of us looked at each other. The only way to turn a wolf safely—and I use the term 'safely' loosely—would be with a piece of moon rock. You'd expose a werewolf to the moon rock just long enough to turn them and have them bite the person you want turned—hopefully not you—then lock the rock back up in its fancy silver box before the werewolf had time to tear everyone to pieces and feast on their insides. It was the only way you could control the timing, something you couldn't do when the full moon was out.

Was there more than one moon rock floating around? Or was the only piece the one that had been buried in Ethan's backyard last year? And if Riah was right, did that mean Samuel was behind it?

Of course Violet and her wilds took this moment to lumber down the stairs join us. Violet beamed when she caught sight of us, motioning us all up for hugs.

She introduced us as she made her rounds, then pointed at her friends. "Grey, Elbie, and Louise."

Grey was older, judging by the color of his hair, which meant he'd been turned once he had it or he was a few hundred years old. Vampires were mortal and did age, just extraordinarily slowly. Louise looked about Violet's age and gave off the same mom vibes with her cozy sweater, while Elbie looked like he could have been in high school with us. His eyes were sunken saucers and his long hair was bound in a messy bun. They were all skeletal, common for wilds who didn't drink as much blood as our skinny vampires did.

"I'm so happy we're doing this," she said as they all sat down.

The waiter came around with another Parrino trio. Violet listened to the descriptions of each as if she hadn't helped build this place with her ex-husband. She sorted out which shot to give to which of her friends, then told them to drink up.

Elbie wrinkled his nose. "He said this was cold."

Patting Elbie's hand, she smiled. "And soothing. You always run hot. Try it."

Louise took hers like a swig of strong alcohol, shaking her head and shivering it down. Grey sipped at his like it might be poison.

"He's cute, Vi." Louise nodded at Ethan. "Looks just like you."

"Eric does too." She strummed her fingers on the table. "He's working tonight, I think. Maybe we can sneak into the kitchen later."

I raised an eyebrow. Eric was still not speaking to her. He would not be pleased.

"Do they talk?" Grey asked, scanning the four of us.

"They do." Violet smiled in our direction. "They just aren't used to sitting in the cellar."

"Doesn't bother me," I lied. It smelled like blood down here. Metallic and cloying.

"Siren, yeah?" Elbie asked Stella, with an uptick of his chin. Ethan stiffened. "What's life like for a siren here in Shady Woods?"

She crossed her arms over her chest and tilted her chin up. "It's delightful. What would you think it'd be?"

He shrugged. "Difficult. It's not water."

"We adapt."

"Everyone adapts, if they have to."

"What's it been like for you?" I asked. "Difficult?"

"Honestly, yeah."

"Then why'd you come?"

"I was lonely." Elbie held my gaze, as if inviting me to do something about it. Riah snaked an arm around my shoulder.

"How'd the four of you find each other?" Ethan asked.

"Samuel," Louise answered. Violet slid her a look and cleared her throat.

The arm of Riah's that was settled around me tightened at Samuel's name. "Why aren't you in L.A. with him?"

Sneaky, I cooed into Riah's head, impressed. He was fishing to find out if Samuel was in L.A., if he might actually be the one behind the moon vacations and Jenny Jones growing a foot, if these celebrities and influencers might actually be abnormals now.

Violet, like any true vampire, didn't show much of a reaction, but her careful nonreaction seemed pretty damning, in and of itself.

"You've been with Samuel?" Ethan asked his mother. "Since you left?"

"No one is as close to him as she is," Louise bragged, a fondness in her gaze as she smiled at Violet with admiration.

I about choked. Samuel had been the one Violet left her family for. Samuel wasn't here. He had the moon rock. The moon rock was most likely with him in L.A. Violet's social media was full of influencers. Because she knew them? No. She couldn't know them. This was ridiculous.

Riah... But I didn't know what to say. He glanced at me.

"What brought the rest of you here?" I asked. "Why did the rest of you choose Shady Woods?"

"Personally, I'm tired," Grey said, finishing his shot with a last sip. "I've been off the grid for too long. The thought of easy feeding and a warm, soft bed..."

Elbie snorted. "Easy feeding is stale feeding."

"If that's how you feel," Ethan said, his voice steel, "you should probably go."

"Wait until you try the blood pie." Violet raised a finger to call the waiter over and ordered two.

Elbie winked at Ethan. "Easy enough to sneak off, take a quick detour to one of those little towns on highway eight, and find a warm body."

"That's not Samuel's plan, Elb." Louise shifted in her seat. "We're trying to make *this* work."

"Samuel's plan?" I echoed quietly. They all looked to me, but didn't answer, so I clarified, "Wilds in Shady is Samuel's plan?"

"It's part of the compromise," Violet said to Elbie, ignoring my question. "Not leaving dead bodies behind. Particularly not in the area to draw any attention. Have you been to the blood bank yet?"

"The live feeds aren't bad," said Grey.

"Not bad if you don't need the wind in your hair."

"You can run for wind in your hair," I muttered as the waiter approached with Violet's order.

"Why are you here," Riah asked, "if you're not willing to give up the hunt?"

Elbie grinned at me. "There are all sorts of ways to soothe a hunting instinct."

"Elbie." Violet said it like she was scolding him, like she'd scolded him before.

"Imagine what it would be like, living like this but able to do it everywhere." Louise slid a piece of the blood pie onto her plate. "Think of how siren tears could advance medicine. Normals would benefit from that as much as they would lose. If there was an understanding between normals and abnormals, we could drink more often and not leave any dead bodies in our wake. That's his plan. It's a win/win really."

"Most wilds are too consumed with survival and staying hidden to have any kind of real life," Grey said. "Why can't they be people too? Why do normals have the monopoly on it?"

"It's what you wanted, that non-life." Ethan stared hard at his mother and the table stilled.

She took a deep breath, pulled a piece of the pie onto her plate, and said, "I wanted us to get to know each other tonight."

"You wanted that?" Ethan challenged. "Or Samuel instructed it?"

Choose me, and you will last, Samuel had said to me last year. *Choose this town, and you will die at the hands of chaos.*

Little did he know, I would never not choose this town.

"I wanted it," she said, like it was a promise. "I wanted my friends and family to get to know each other."

With a sigh, I stood to reach for a piece of the blood pie. Slumping back in my chair, I shoved it into my mouth, one huge bite at a time. It probably looked like my favorite food, but really, I was agitated.

"Riah." Violet smiled at him while watching me eat. "Ethan says you like to run. Maybe you could take Elbie out sometime?"

"What else do you like to do, Elbie?" I asked. Besides run and hunt and not 'be lonely.'

And so the conversation turned to all the things they didn't have access to in the wild that they might like to try. Soon enough, Grey and Louise seemed much more approachable, but I wasn't sure anything could do that for Elbie.

The four of them left first—it seemed harder for them to sit still—and once they'd disappeared up the steps, Riah drummed his fingertips on the table. "A dead body was found between Pulaski and Crivitz last week. Unexplained blood loss. I didn't think it was connected until now."

"It's always connected," I muttered. "Next time, just remind me in the beginning—everything is always connected."

Riah stood, seemingly in a daze. "Let's take the tunnels home."

Stella raised an eyebrow at him. "I'm not taking the tunnels home."

The tunnel network was built at the start of Shady Woods so the vampires didn't have to be out in the sun. The only houses with access were the founding vampire's homes. This meant that technically, Ethan was the only one of us who could get home from here. Granted, I did live right next door to him, but Stella was in the opposite direction and Riah somewhere in the middle.

"Fine. I really just need Grace."

"For what?"

"I can't say."

"Think you'll be able to find your way without me?" Ethan asked. "I'll drive Stella home and you and Grace can do... whatever it is you're going to do."

"Why wouldn't we be able to find our way without you?" I asked.

"It's dark."

I held up my phone.

"And unmarked."

I looked to Riah.

"We have to try. Come on." And then he was striding toward the cellar bar and the back corner beyond it.

I glanced at Ethan, who shrugged, and Stella, who tossed me a wary smile.

Right. Well, good thing I trusted Riah more than anyone else in this town.

He turned to wait for me. As I approached, he offered me a hand. I took it and he led me into a thin passageway. My shoulders brushed the walls as I shuffled forward.

As he turned on the flashlight on his phone, I asked, "Will you tell me what we're doing now?"

Shining the light behind me as if the bartender in the cellar might be able to hear, he replied. "A little bit further."

After what felt like a block, we came to an intersection. "The old town council is meeting tonight. They meet when they can—not very often—and only decide at the last minute. My dad was considering having us come, having you share your memories of Samuel and how he controlled the wolf and the box, but was worried it still felt like a conspiracy theory."

"And after what we heard tonight, you don't think it'll still feel that way."

"Right. This way."

We went straight, then walked and walked and walked.

"No one comes down here anymore?" I asked.

"Not really. That's why they picked it to meet."

"Did you tell them we were coming?"

"Yeah. I'm just not sure what kind of service they have."

"Great."

He squeezed my hand. "Don't worry, I'll go first."

Eventually, I detected the faintest light from up ahead, along with an echoed whisper of voices. It grew louder and brighter, and soon the narrow tunnel opened onto a larger space with battery-powered lanterns hanging on the walls. The seven members of the old council sat in a circle on wooden benches. They hushed as we entered and Mr. Jenkins stood.

"You all know my son, Riah," he said. "And this is Grace James, William and Anna's daughter." But he looked a little confused.

"I'm sorry to interrupt," Riah said. "But we have some news."

"Grace is a dendrite," his dad explained. "So she can share some memories with us."

One of the councilmembers nodded. "Memories are best. We'd appreciate that."

Riah squeezed my hand. Yes. Right. I probably smelled a bit freaked out. But there was no reason to be nervous. Cobwebs weren't scary and the scurrying feet of rodents wasn't scary. The scrapings on the walls that looked like a monster unleashed itself here? I'd seen worse. The new council finding out we were working against them? When they had allies such as wilds and Samuel and others who didn't mind draining bodies in the woods?

I swallowed hard.

"I've been a bit confused about how Riah explained that moon rock," another spoke up. "It'll be nice to see it more clearly."

"I'm sorry to bring you into this, Grace," Riah's dad said, as if he'd orchestrated us being there. "But you have more memories of Samuel than your parents do, and I didn't want to bring any more people into this than necessary."

"Of course."

Everyone stared at me and Mr. Jenkins motioned for us to take a seat.

"Oh!" Okay, right. I moved to sit, pulling Riah with me. He kept hold of my hand as we settled, and his arm landed on my lap.

Why was I freaking out? Just because we were underground and the air felt trapped, like I imagined it would in a coffin?

"Whenever you're ready," Riah's dad said.

With a hard swallow, I closed my eyes, pulling my first memories of Samuel up from the recesses of my mind. All of the memories of Samuel, a slideshow. The memory of Aster breaking the box open and what that almost did to her and Riah. The one of my father slicing off a werewolf's head before it could sink its teeth into me. How that same werewolf had snapped my dog's neck like he was a green bean. Full body shivers ensued, and Riah closed whatever space had been lingering between us. The vision wavered, in my mind and in theirs, and then I sent them most of the dinner conversation we'd just had with Violet and her friends.

When my memories faded back into the recesses of my mind, I felt chilled to the bone. Too much of Samuel all at once or too much energy leeching from my brain, I couldn't tell, but the shivers didn't fade. The fear didn't either, from that night in our back hall. The pool of blood on the floor. How close we'd been to losing one or all of us.

Springing up, needing to get away from it, I ran back the way we'd come. Of course I had no idea where I was going and soon it was pitch black, so I waited for Riah while telling myself I was stronger now. I could defend myself now, not only against werewolves, but also vampires. Sparring with Jeremy was helping me become a more diverse fighter.

When Riah finally found me, I turned to hug him, but my arms couldn't get up and around him because of the narrow hallway, so I ended up face first in his neck. We stood like that for a while, him not moving and me trying not to cry. Failing not to cry.

I took deep breaths of him, filled myself with this person who could always center me, and told myself it was only the deep tunnel and its mood that had me so exposed.

"They're taking it all to the Elder Board," Riah whispered, loose fingertips at my waist. The Elder Board consisted of the oldest vampires on the planet. They made sure things never got out of hand. "Samuel will not get away with this."

Chapter Nine

Sofia Happened

Jeremy stood at attention in front of my parents at the base of the stairs, his spine straight and every tendon rigid.

"Dad, knock it off. We're just going as friends." It was pretty cute though, how nervous he seemed. Christian had handled my dad's interrogations much better.

Yellow means friends, Grace, my mom pointed out. *He didn't bring you a yellow corsage.*

I rolled my eyes to her. Certainly, the whole of Shady Woods didn't follow what rose colors meant the way humans did.

"Stand in front of the fireplace," she instructed. "Let me take a picture."

Jeremy's eyes cut to me, as if he wasn't sure he was allowed to stand down. I smiled at him. "At ease, soldier."

He glanced back toward my dad, who still had his arms crossed and his weight on his heels.

"Dad! He's been around for weeks now. It's not like you've never seen him before." We sparred in the backyard as much as we did in Ethan's basement, depending on the weather, and my mom had even sent him home with dinner one night.

I looped an arm through Jeremy's and walked him to the fireplace. "Yellow roses mean friends," I whispered. "My mom thought you should know, for next time."

"Coral means desire and fascination."

I looked up at him, eyebrows raised, and this was when he chose to relax. He met my surprise with a grin and my mom snapped a handful of pictures.

"Um…"

He laughed, sweeping up the five blankets I'd stacked on the couch. "We're bringing all of these?"

I nodded, grabbing the bag of winter clothes. Both were for Nora's after-party bonfire. In February. With fresh snow on the ground. Sometimes I questioned the collective sanity of Shady Woods but apparently it was a thing.

"Great. Let's go. I'm starving."

Slipping into my puffy marshmallow coat for warmth, I followed him out to his van. He moved at vampire speed to dump the blankets and open the door for me before I got there.

I shook my head at him.

"What?" he asked innocently, brushing back his hair, which was mostly short but long enough at the front that it fell in his eyes a bit.

"Desire and fascination," I muttered.

He winked, closed the door, and came around to the driver's side.

We were meeting at Parrino's for pizza, which was somewhat ironic since that had been the location of our terrible date freshman year, and I spotted my friends from the sidewalk before we even walked in. They were easy to spot, since we'd all chosen some form of pink for Valentine's Day, and Aster's bright choice was like a beacon out the front window. A color Stella could never pull off as pale as she was, which maybe explained why she'd chosen a pink on the opposite end of the spectrum. I was in a dusty rose tulle skirt and black cropped tee. There had been only one light pink choice for men's shirts at the boutique, so Ethan, Riah, Christian, and Jeremy all matched. Riah's orange tie didn't look great with his shirt.

Kiara and Aster had yellow corsages, while Stella's was red. I slid my arm behind my back as we approached.

Even so, Christian showed up in my head. *A coral rose? You know what that means?*

I rolled my eyes. *I'm surprised Jeremy does.*

Who do you think taught him?

Right. The romantic.

It ended up being a whole lot less awkward than I thought it would be, as long as Jeremy kept his hands off me. Whenever he nudged me, or threw an arm casually around my shoulder, Christian would stiffen and clear his throat. Everyone seemed to notice when it happened, except Jeremy, who chattered over whatever hiccup Christian's posturing had rent through the conversation.

Still, I was able to breathe a bit easier at the dance when Jeremy led me onto the dance floor, away from everyone else. He held me with a few inches between us, one arm around my waist and the other holding my hand by our shoulders.

A smile grew on his face, and just when it started to feel uncomfortable, he leaned down to whisper in my ear, "You are the most beautiful girl here."

I rolled my eyes. "I hardly try anymore. A girl can't really compete with the sirens." Stella was all legs and blonde hair, her facial features perfectly sculpted.

"You don't need to."

"Clearly you're just blowing smoke up my—"

He cut me off with his lips. On mine. Contact that I wasn't expecting, even after the coral rose. I squeaked softly, which was much better than spitting him off the way I had freshman year. His mouth spread into a smile against mine before he slowly got back to the task at hand, maybe making sure I had time to stop things if I wanted to.

I didn't want to. And not only because I was slightly frozen in shock. This meant he settled in for a seriously serious kiss.

Jeremy kissed everyone. And the rumors were true, he was great at it. Of course I'd fall into it and get distracted for a moment. Who wouldn't? Besides, the very fact that he kissed everyone meant I didn't have to take this maturation of our relationship too seriously, right? He never got serious, and I didn't want serious, so we could fight and kiss and when he lost interest like he always did, maybe by then I'd actually be ready to date someone.

When he pulled away, I muttered, "Dang, you're a good kisser." Now I understood why Charlie always said kissing was meant to be spread around.

He grinned. "You're welcome for the do-over."

I burst out laughing. He jerked me closer to him and dipped his head to my ear, which thankfully I couldn't see, because I was certain, tall as he was, that he was bending at an extreme vampire angle.

"I'm going to kiss you again, better than that even, and you're going to try to shock me."

"So this is just a training exercise?"

"What does your corsage tell you?"

I pulled back to smirk at him. "I'm impressed with how much your game has improved since freshman year."

"Good. Because for this to work, I need you to be feeling me like I'm feeling you."

I swallowed at the intensity of his gaze. It made me want to squirm a little. I wasn't completely comfortable with this turn of events. Kissing, maybe. Desire and fascination? Not so much.

"Passion can run pretty deep. Since anger and frustration haven't yet been able to pull any output from you, I thought a little passion might."

I wasn't convinced my feelings for Jeremy were anything but shallow. They were warm, sure, but not very deep. Then again, the way he was looking at me? No wonder people got swept away. The way he was looking at me, I *wanted* to get swept away.

"Okay." I nodded, tilting my head up to him.

When he kissed me this time, there was not one ounce of question in it. His lips were confident and deliberate, insistent, like he'd waited too long for this. Though I knew that couldn't be true, that he didn't attach himself to anyone, it was all-encompassing. I sank into it, sliding my fingers up to his jaw. I drew on the molten heat in my belly, on the swoon-worthiness of the kiss, the languid chords of the song playing, the citrus undertone of Jeremy's cologne, on my body pressed against his. I imagined weaving it all together until it built enough that I wanted more from him, even though I knew I didn't really want more from him. I pushed all that out until my mind reached my fingertips, there against his skin.

Opening my eyes, I didn't see anything, no blue or white sparks, no fuzz. He was still kissing me, deeper now, but before I could try again, we were ripped apart and Christian took a swing at Jeremy, almost smacking me in the process.

Aster was on Christian in an instant, pulling him off and holding him back. Jeremy leveled a perfectly serene vampire gaze at Christian while touching down on his now split lip.

"You're supposed to be my friend," Christian choked out, his face bent, unable to look at me.

"I'm training her, Chris. Trying to get her shock to work."

"Bullshit. You just can't let it go that she didn't fall for you like everyone else."

Jeremy's forehead furrowed. "That has nothing to do with it."

"No? Then what does it have to do with?"

He shrugged, his gaze flitting to me and then back to Christian. "I like her, okay?"

"You're my best friend."

"Dude. She was mine first, if you want to be like that."

"Dude," Aster echoed, eyes narrowed on Jeremy. "Don't be an asshat."

Jeremy threw up his hands. "Everyone dates my ex-girlfriends without even thinking about it. Why doesn't anyone care when it's me who might be hurt?"

"You have dated the entire school," Aster said. "If your friends stayed away from everyone you've dated, there'd be no one left. Plus, you don't care enough about anyone to care who they date after."

"Is that really what you think of me?"

All three of us eyeballed him. "We think you care about your friends," I said.

"Fine." He waved his hand. "Think whatever you want."

Christian lunged for Jeremy again, but Jeremy was faster this time and stepped cleanly out of the way. Aster caught the back of Christian's shirt before he fell, jerking him upright with her werewolf strength. I heard an aching, desperate, *Grace, please,* echo through my head as she strode with him across the gym.

I stepped forward to wipe the dark smear of vampire blood off Jeremy's skin.

"I don't know if I can do this to him," I said.

"Do what? We're just training. Honestly, he should be glad it's me and not someone you might be serious about."

Fair point. Gingerly, I touched the soft discoloration beneath his lip. His skin was already thoroughly woven back together, the edge of his mouth slightly swollen but probably not for long. "If we're just training, then stop looking at me like that."

"Like I'm going to kiss you again?"

"Right."

He smirked. "Until you get any output from it, I think we need to try harder."

Behind me in a vampire instant, he slid his arm around my waist and settled his mouth to my neck the way he did to end a fight, to say he won. Only this time, it wasn't just the soft whisper of his lips, but a firmly pressed kiss. Christian was in my direct line of sight, folded over in a chair with his elbows on his knees, head hanging.

Clearing my throat, I held my hand up, the blood I'd wiped from his face dry and beet purple. "I should go clean this up and maybe we should save the training for my backyard." Or at least not rub it in Christian's face.

I'm so sorry for Emily. Christian's voice filled my mind. It was the first time this apology felt real, as if he were taking full responsibility for it and not blaming it on his dream. *I can't even imagine what this would have felt like had it happened back then.*

Then I was slammed with emotion. I wasn't sure Christian was doing it on purpose, but his feelings were cycling through me: loss, fear, need, love, desire, heartache, denial, hope.

It was too much. I had to get away. And I had blood on my hand.

I hurried to the nearest bathroom, willing myself not to cry, at least not until I got there.

The emotions I wanted to cry over were his, not mine. I didn't own them anymore. It was over for me.

Barging into the bathroom, I stopped short before I could make it to the sink. Sofia, Emily, Addison Jacobs, and Elbie (the wild who'd been at dinner with us) were huddled around a senior dendrite I hardly knew. I couldn't really blame Addison for ending up with Sofia—had I been turned against my will into a vampire, I'd have a lot of rage too. And rage was something Sofia seemed to understand.

Sofia's arm was wrapped around Elbie. His hand hung over her shoulder, bony fingers with huge knuckles, veins almost visible from where I stood against the door.

"What's up?" I asked casually, while categorizing all the things wrong with this picture: boy in the girl's bathroom, wild at a high school dance, dendrite alone with four blood-sucking vampires. Sofia and Emily were always bad news, but now Sofia and a wild?

"Shoo, Grace," Sofia said, stepping in front of the senior. "Find another bathroom."

Moving to the sink to wash my hands, I caught a glimpse of silver in the mirror. Silver often meant siren tears but this time it meant a knife.

My hands stilled under the faucet as the senior sliced through the skin of his own shoulder. This way, without vampire teeth sinking into tissue, there was no chance you'd turn into one. Emily nudged Addison, and Addison put her mouth to the cut.

A suckling noise brought me back to freshman year, when Ethan drank from a raccoon to more quickly heal a gunshot wound. I shivered, sweeping back out of the bathroom as quickly as I could. Hands still wet, I ran blindly into Riah as I reached the gym.

"What happened?" he asked. "You smell... not okay."

Sofia happened. They're drinking live in the bathroom at a high school dance.

Chapter Ten

Bonfire and Ice

Riah grabbed Jeremy, Stella, and Ethan. The five of us left right away.

The snow had been cleared from a section of frozen lake in Nora's backyard, and half our grade was already there. The moon was bright and the sky clear, plus the huge bonfire at the shore lent enough light to find your way around.

By the time Stella and I had changed into warmer clothes and winter layers, Aster was standing with Riah, Ethan, and Jeremy.

"Christian went home," she told me. "Said he's over high school."

I frowned.

"Don't worry. He smelled okay. I'll check on him tomorrow." Stella squeezed my shoulder, then led Ethan down to the ice.

"You tell Kiara you were leaving the dance?" Aster asked Riah.

His mouth dropped open as if he were going to say something, but nothing came out.

She rolled her eyes. "You're as bad as Jeremy."

"Hey." Jeremy sidled up next to me. "I've been an excellent date this time around. Yeah?"

"Yeah," I agreed.

Riah pulled his phone out to text Kiara, and we left him for the roasting table. Marshmallows, chocolate bars, peanut butter cups, graham crackers, and roasting sticks sat next to jars of red lumps floating in a pink liquid.

Aster plucked one of the lumps out and popped it in her mouth. I wrinkled my nose. "Some kind of tongue," she reported.

"Hopefully not human," Jeremy muttered, lifting the jar to sniff it.

She wobbled her head back and forth as if thinking about it, then swallowed. "Pretty sure it's badger, though I haven't had much badger in my life."

"Why would you think it could be human?" I asked.

They turned to me.

"There was a bunch in the cooler," Aster said, very quietly.

The cooler was a special wolf section at the grocery store that held all sorts of fresh meat. "There was a shipment of *human meat?*"

Aster made an I'm-very-sorry-to-be-the-one-to-tell-you-this face, and Jeremy reached a hand out to steady me. Pushing him away, I stumbled to the nearest chair. It squeaked as it settled in the snow, and I tucked my boots under it, resting my elbows on my knees and trying to get my head to stop spinning. Jeremy crouched down next to me. "You okay?"

I waved him away and shook my head. Not okay, but I needed a moment. He nodded and returned to Aster. I could feel them watching me.

A little later, Riah set a chair in front of me and sat down so his knees touched mine. "Rough night, huh?"

I heard the catch in his voice and looked up into his eyes. He was sad, but his face lacked the righteous indignation that usually came on the heels of something like this, which meant he'd known about it and already grappled with his disgust.

It felt like we were two steps closer to chaos—vampires drinking fresh from willing participants in public and werewolves buying human meat as a delicacy. I was having a hard time swallowing, like I had a marshmallow stuck in my throat. *Choose this town and you will die at the hands of chaos,* Samuel had said. But how would choosing him look any different?

Riah's hand dangled between us. Sliding my glove off, I linked my fingers in his, needing an anchor. He rubbed his thumb across my skin for a moment and then pulled back. Curling my fingers into my palm, I closed my eyes.

The only thing I could do about it, to feel like I had any control in the matter, was train harder. The rest was up to the adults, the old council, and Aster's dad, who'd been tasked to reach the elders, to tell them about our suspicions of Samuel in Hollywood.

I was slightly disappointed in myself, that after all this time living among people whose wild counterparts had no problem feasting on my blood and muscle, I still couldn't stomach this news. Of course something like this would be happening somewhere. When and where it could, supply met demand. That's what it did. Was there any more reliable tenet in the world?

"They say they harvest it from already dead bodies, that no one is killed for the purpose of butchering and selling the meat."

My throat got tight, my nose tingled, and tears gathered in my eyes. Riah curled forward, almost as if he'd wrap himself around me as a shield if he could, and his hand slid back into mine. A point of contact, a physical distraction.

I closed my eyes and focused on that, waiting for it to relax me. Only, it didn't happen. Instead of settling, every nerve in my body stood at attention. It was the strangest sensation, being so *aware*—the raging fire and its shadows dancing around us, the snow and the ice. The cold on my cheeks, Riah's knee against mine, his steady breathing.

Events of the night washed over me—Jeremy's mouth on mine, his lips on my neck, Christian's aching, the offering in the bathroom, the human meat that might as well be me in the grocery store, the absolute hopelessness of it all—and I opened my eyes to look at Riah, my gaze landing on his lips. His face.

I breathed out slow and steady, trying to channel my sadness, anger, and fear before they tugged me under, before they made me cry. I would not cry here. And in the attempt to shove it all away, I felt a buzz at my fingertips.

We both straightened, eyes wide on the blue fizz jumping between us.

My heart pounded, loud and rapid. Riah slid his hand over mine and wound it around, fingers sliding past fingers and skin whispering to skin. The moment suspended itself.

Thump, thump. Thump, thump.

"That's incredible," he muttered.

I watched his face, marveling over me, and it happened again without me trying—tiny sparks, as if they were jumping up to meet him. The soft blue fuzz turned quickly from spikes and sparks to a hazy fog that dissipated to nothing. A few bounced onto the snow with a sizzle. Like a sparkler. My fingers were sparklers.

Riah offered up his other hand and we sat, connected. He kept looking back and forth between our hands and my eyes, and then he'd take a deep breath in. Was he reading me? Why would he be reading me? What was there to read that wasn't obvious?

Standing so quickly that I knocked over my chair, I took off, bumping into Kiara on the way. She'd been crying, and I should care, but I just needed to get away. It was dark and late and the nearest place I could think to go was out on the lake.

There were tracks through the snow in every direction. I knew this was a thing they did, walk the ice, but it had always made me nervous. Tonight I was driven by need, by the urge to escape.

Driven into what I had previously thought was dangerous because my everyday life kept ramping up the stakes.

I stopped when I was far enough out that the noise was small behind me, muffled by the trees so thick on the shore. Sinking to my knees, I let the darkness envelop me, the moon bright and high but not full, and rested my fists against my eyes to keep the tears at bay. The wind tried to comfort me, soft and forgiving, whispering across the vast empty space.

When I felt a little more in control, I gazed up at the stars piercing the sky, the constellations as clear as I'd ever seen them.

"Do you ever think you know something, but still have a hard time believing it?"

I startled at Riah's voice. "I wouldn't think that would happen to a wolf," I replied.

He gave me the gloves I'd left by the bonfire. "Sometimes people act differently than they smell. It's like getting mixed messages but you know the person doesn't mean to give them, so you can't really blame them for playing games. Nose could always be wrong, too—"

"Could it though?"

He shrugged. Because no, it couldn't. "Plus, I never want to come off as weird or intrusive, by knowing too much."

"I like that I don't have to explain what I'm feeling, that you just get me. There's a lot of comfort in that."

"Comfort." He took a deep breath in and looked away.

"Is this about Kiara?" I asked.

"No."

"She seemed pretty upset."

"She should be."

I studied him, his attention on the lake now. "Hey, you okay?"

"I feel like a total shit, but yeah, I'm fine. You?"

"Not at all. Why do you feel like a total shit?"

"Because I chose you over my date. Left her at the dance. Hardly gave her another thought."

I reached for his hand, but it was in his coat pocket. He left it there, and my arm flapped at my side. "I'm sorry." I wasn't exactly sure what I was apologizing for. A lot of things, maybe. That I knew what it felt like to be tugged toward him while in a relationship, and how hard it was to balance both. That I let myself get so upset he had to focus on me instead of his girlfriend.

He shook his head. "I'd do it again."

"If I hadn't been upset..."

"If you hadn't been upset, I still would've rather been with you. I'd always rather be with you."

My hands filled with pop rocks and I lost my focus. Turning my palms up, I confirmed that I was doing it again. Telelectrical output. Just like that.

Riah stared at the light, but also seemed to be staring past it. "I've figured it out."

"Figured what out?"

"Love."

"Yeah?"

"Wanna hear?"

"Of course."

He cleared his throat. "I think there's an emptiness when the people you love aren't around. A missing piece."

"And when they are around?"

"You feel happy, of course. Sated. Content. Like all is right with the world."

I grinned at his use of the word sated. He must have spent a lot of time thinking about this. "That's lovely, Riah."

Footsteps crunched on the snow behind us. Jeremy slid a hand around my waist and kissed the side of my head. It was awkward, what with the puffy winter coats, but Jeremy had long arms. Riah hunched his shoulders over like he was cold, nodded, and turned to walk back to the party.

"Aster said you needed a moment," Jeremy said. "So I gave you a few."

"I'm okay," I lied.

"Wanna know how I forget the injustices of the world?"

"I imagine you kiss them away."

He smirked. "Not what I was going to say."

"What, then?"

"I make myself stronger. More formidable."

"You train?"

"With my dad's axes."

I raised an eyebrow. The axes his dad stocked at the gas station used to freak me out, before I realized that was their very purpose, to be a deterrent.

"How about we add some axe throwing to your training regimen?" he asked.

I raised both eyebrows.

"Is that a yes?"

"Oh, that's a yes."

Chapter Eleven

You Two Need a Room?

It took a few more weeks before I actually got my hands on an axe.

"A handmade axe," Jeremy stressed, as he held it out to me.

We were in his backyard. His house was in a pocket of forest between the edge of town and the truck stop, his driveway a narrow dirt lane I didn't think I'd have noticed if it weren't plowed. The way the trees leaned into each other overhead made it feel like we'd created our own tunnel as we'd driven through.

It was sunny and warmish. I assumed this was why we walked around the house instead of through. That, or he wasn't ready for me to meet his mom or see his room. Very possible. Fine by me.

"It's beautiful," I whispered, because he hadn't let go and it seemed this was what he was waiting for. The axe's handle was thick and scrolled with a design that he'd carved on his own.

"It was my first." He gazed at it more tenderly than I'd ever seen him look at a girl.

"Are you going to show me how to use this thing, or do you two need a room?"

His lip turned up on the right, a half smirk. Setting the axe on the rack carefully, he patted it, then moved behind me to point at the boards nailed to each tree. They had human-shaped outlines, a paper doll army come to life and marching our way.

"You're aiming for the chest. Midrange is the easiest hit. We'll start you double-handed, weak leg forward." He handed me an axe, then stood next to me to demonstrate. "Hold it like this, bring it back over your head, all the way, don't be afraid to rest it against your back. When you throw, shift your weight forward, swing it over your head, and let go about shoulder height. Whether it hits higher or lower depends on when you let go, but like I said, the chest is your best bet." Jeremy stepped back and waited.

"Now?" I asked. "Already?"

"It's not that hard. Give it a try."

I got in position and rocked a bit, but was having a hard time pulling the trigger, so to speak. I kept imagining how if I let go too late, it might come back at my feet.

"Okay, here. Let me show you." He picked up his baby, kissing the blade as he lined himself up on the other side of the rack, and tossed it over his head. It landed in the wood with a satisfying smack and shook the tree out.

"Wow."

"I know, I don't look that strong." He winked. "Your turn."

Okay. Left leg forward, elbows up, back of the axe resting between my shoulder blades. One, two, *three.* It slid with a soft thud onto the grass a few feet from the target. I rolled my eyes.

"And you look stronger than that." He grinned. "This time, throw it like you mean it."

In the time it took me to line up, ready myself, and throw one axe, Jeremy had thrown five from the rack. Then we walked to the targets, collected the axes, and queued back up for another round.

By the time the sun had sunk behind the trees, I'd been hitting the target more often than not and taking more and more time between to watch the different ways he threw. Not two-handed. Never two-handed. He threw it with one arm, he threw it sideways, he threw it like a frisbee, and he even threw it by holding onto the dull end of the blade. My shoulders ached when we stopped, and Jeremy wind-milled his arms with the kind of flexibility only a vampire could manage.

"Hungry?" he asked.

"Famished, actually."

Grabbing his favorite axe, he held it low, fingers at the far end of the handle, and led me to the back door. There were three hooks on the wall, two empty until he replaced his next to the other. Three spots for everyone's favorite axe, maybe. "Are you an only child?"

"Sure am." He patted the handle once before leaving it there, then turned into the kitchen to fling open the fridge and drink a few gulps of cold blood before putting it in the microwave to warm the rest. While it heated, he opened a bottom cabinet and checked the date on a bag of chips. "Expired. Let me take you somewhere."

"You don't have to do that."

"I want to."

An alarm screeched and I jumped. Jeremy calmly strode across the room and down a few steps to their family room, which was full of old TVs.

Security cameras, I realized, once he switched them on. Between them all, they covered every angle of the truck stop, inside and out. A car was passing on the street but didn't turn in. As it moved out of the last screen, the alarm went off on its own.

"That's got to get annoying."

Jeremy flipped the TVs off. "You get used to it."

"Is that so your dad can come home once in a while?" The truck stop was open twenty-four hours.

"It was. But he doesn't."

"It's also so we can help if needed."

I spun around to find the other half of this "we." A woman who had to be Jeremy's mom stood on the first step that led back to the kitchen, arms crossed.

She smiled at me. "Jeremy has never once brought a girl home. Not since Aster broke his heart."

"Mom."

She grinned, which did a lot to relax me, because otherwise she might have been the most intimidating person I'd ever met. Taller than Jeremy, with dark hair wound in a knot at the base of her neck, she wore a black blazer that closed in the front with three strips of chain. It was clear she wore nothing beneath it. Her sleeves looked cinched up to her elbows, almost pushed, but as if they were sewn that way, and her forearms were corded with muscle. The only jewelry she wore was her wedding band, which held a fat golden bee lifting its wings, about to take off. Her pleated olive green pants were loose and bunched into black, steel-toed combat boots, and she wore a small axe on her belt.

Mrs. Holmes reached a hand out for me to shake. "Nice to meet you," she said. "You can call me Althea."

"Nice to meet you, too. I'm Grace."

Handshake complete, she crossed her arms again. "You had some nice form out there."

"Thank you. Your son is a good teacher."

"He does have a way about him. He gets that from his father." She pursed her lips as if this "way" wasn't always a good thing, but she was so amazingly badass I didn't care if the air had skewed awkward. She gave me hope that someday I could be that tough and that cool too.

"I love your jacket," I told her.

"Thank you."

"She made it herself." A note of pride ran through Jeremy's voice, but as quickly as it came, he was bounding up the steps next to her. "We're going to get Grace something edible."

"After you put that half gallon back in the fridge."

Jeremy hung his head and swept into the kitchen to pull the blood out of the microwave and put it back.

His mom winked at me, then disappeared up the other set of stairs that I imagined led to their bedrooms.

"Your dad never comes home?" I asked, once we were in his van.

He didn't answer and the ride to town was quiet. It had me reaching for his hand, worried I'd upset him. It was hard to believe, his dad never coming home, because his mom was incredible. I played with his squishy vampire fingers a little, bending them this way and that, having a new appreciation for them after watching him swing and aim an axe.

Soon, though, I let go, not wanting to give him the wrong idea. Not that all the kissing of the last few weeks hadn't already done that. It must have been what his mom said about him never bringing a girl home that worried me. I was pretty sure he'd only brought me home to train, but just in case.

By the time I'd ordered and we were settled in a booth at Al's, Jeremy seemed back to himself.

"Nice work today. You're a natural."

"If only it were easier to carry an axe around."

He shrugged one shoulder. "I could make you a belt for that."

I smiled. "So many hidden talents, Jeremy. Axe carving and leather work?"

"I'm a craftsman at heart, what can I say."

"Does your whole family make things?" His dad and his axes, his mom and her clothes...

"I guess. But let's not talk about my family."

I sucked milkshake through a straw as he peered at his reflection in his phone and futzed with his hair. "Okay," I said. "What do you want to talk about?"

And the answer to that, of course, was my training. He'd become more intense than Aster, which was saying something. Aster was the highest of over-achievers and took every goal seriously. Jeremy, I'd thought, was much more laid back, but he did seem to enjoy having a mission. In fact, right now, he was texting Riah on my phone, asking him if they could coordinate my running with my training schedule, for better payoff.

His head was down and his shoulders bent as he added my new running times, axe throwing schedule, and sparring regimen into the calendar on my phone that my mom had been trying to get me to use my entire life. This meant I was the one who saw the cops flying into the parking lot with their lights on and siren off.

I kicked Jeremy under the table. He looked up as the officer walked in and over to the counter.

"I need Al." The officer twisted his hands and Jeremy leaned back in his seat, tipping the chair on its back legs to get a better look.

When Al appeared from the kitchen, the officer looked down at his feet. "We got word about an hour ago that they picked Nehemiah up."

"The Sentinel?"

"No, sir. The state troopers."

"For what?"

"Someone's been draining bodies in the area."

"Miah isn't a vampire, Pete."

"They don't know that, sir. We tried to get to him first, tried to intercept, but failed. He's in Peshtigo and we're working on getting him transferred but it's not looking good. They found him with a fourth victim. I'm not sure what we'll be able to do."

Nehemiah is not a villain, I muttered in Jeremy's head.

Jeremy settled his chair back to the floor. Reaching for my hands across the table, he brought them to his lips and kissed my knuckles. "You know him well?"

Well enough to know he wants to save people, not kill them.

The officer patted the counter. "We'll keep you posted but I wanted to tell you in person."

"Is there anything I can do?" Al asked.

"Sit tight. We can't push too hard or draw attention, but we'll get some eyes on the ground. We'll get it figured out."

The cop left and Al shooed us out the door to close early for the night.

Chapter Twelve

We Just Did Something

I burst through Ethan's front door, Jeremy on my heels.

I'd been blabbering since we got in his van, and though I think he'd meant to drop me off after dinner, he might have been worried for my sanity.

Mr. Parrino lifted a hand from his chair in the living room in greeting. I nodded at him as I passed and hurried down to the basement to fill Riah, Ethan, and Stella in, ending with, "We have to do something."

"Who are we to do something?" Stella asked.

"*Four* bodies now?" As if Riah couldn't believe he'd missed any.

"It sounds like the police *are* doing something," Ethan said.

"Our police can't explain to the state troopers that it's physically impossible for a wolf to drain a body, thus proving his innocence."

"What if he was there with Reilly?"

"Who cares if he was there with Reilly? If Reilly did it, Nehemiah didn't."

"What do you have in mind?" asked Jeremy.

I stopped pacing. "I don't know. Anyone ever break someone out of jail?"

Riah snorted.

"How are we the right choice to break someone out of jail?" Stella asked.

"Maybe if we were *all* as strong as a wolf, fast as a vampire, charming as a siren, and could place thoughts like a dendrite," Ethan said. "But it's too risky as is."

"It's too risky anyway!" Riah cried. "Hell no!"

"I have axes in my van," Jeremy offered.

"If we wait, he's going to be moved into a bigger facility," I pointed out. "Right now, they're still holding him at the police station. Way less people to manage."

"Listen to you, talking of managing humans, as if we're gods who have any right to manage them."

I ignored that. Riah knew it would push a button, but I didn't have time to care. The injustice of it, the fact that the proof was there but we couldn't offer it up, had me so shaken I couldn't let it go. It wouldn't be feasible, us against a large facility with inmates and guards, etc., which was why we had to do something tonight.

Stella's charm, my placing thoughts, Ethan's speed, Riah's strength if it came down to it... We had to try.

An hour later, Jeremy, Riah, and I were bounding up the steps with the plan to head out there and at least poke around. Walk in and see how many people were actually in the building, maybe try to see Nehemiah in case there was anything he knew that could help us help him. Visiting hours didn't seem to be a thing in holding, so I hoped it wouldn't be too late. If it were, I was ready to spend the night and visit him in the morning. If for nothing else but to reassure him that Shady police were working on it.

Riah was still adamantly against the whole idea but also refused to let us go without him. And since I was determined to go, he was in.

The situation in the kitchen, however, stopped me in my tracks.

Sofia sat at Ethan's kitchen table, head in her hands, while Elbie leaned against the counter with a smile on his face. Violet wiped blood off her chin, expression pinched.

"Why are you here?" I asked Sofia.

She looked up at me, expression weary and soft rather than pointed and harsh like it usually was. "Violet said it was a safe place."

"Why do you need a safe place?"

"We just did something."

"What did you do?"

She looked away, as if it might actually pain her.

Elbie patted his stomach. "We drank a body."

Sofia shot a look at him.

"What's the problem?" he asked. "I thought we did it to save your friend."

"He's not my friend."

Elbie rolled his eyes. "Fine. Then I thought we did it because someone was unfairly detained and your sense of justice was too strong."

I snorted. "Sofia's sense of justice?"

Riah pushed past me. "Detained?"

"Is this about Nehemiah?" Jeremy asked.

"Wait." The pieces settled in my head. "You *killed* someone?"

"Shut up, Grace!" Sofia shouted, as if she had a conscience. "Shut up, okay?"

Elbie moved to where Sofia sat and began to knead her shoulders from behind. As if all it took after killing someone—or watching someone die—was a little massage to ease the mind.

"Another dead body while he was locked up was the only way to prove his innocence," Elbie said. "You should be thanking us."

"You know who did it?" Riah asked, rounding on Violet. "Did one of you do it?"

She set the bloody washcloth down. "I'm sorry, Riah. I know how you feel about this. But when they came to me, I couldn't argue that it was the only way to get an innocent werewolf freed."

"So he's out?" Jeremy asked.

Violet turned to him. "Sofia called the station and reported having seen another body as soon as we were out of town limits. It shouldn't take long for them to find it. Once they do, once they realize that poor wolf was in custody at the time, they should let him go."

Sofia set her head back in her hands. "He looked vicious. I'm trying to tell myself he was vicious."

I gaped at her. At how I could tell she was distraught. Sofia of all people. Distraught enough that under different circumstances, I could see comforting her. Except she'd *killed* someone. They'd killed someone. I didn't care that Elbie—and maybe even Violet—saw it as the natural order of things. I didn't care it was something that happened out there, where wilds roamed. And I'm not sure Sofia did either.

Rushing to the sink, I braced myself against the counter and threw up.

Chapter Thirteen

Not Okay

Riah slammed into his seat at lunch on Monday. "The Elder Board is missing."

"What do you mean?" Ethan asked. "How can they be missing?"

"The compound is empty. Like a ghost town. A note was pinned to the inner sanctum." He opened his phone to relay it exactly. "'We are gone, forever away. Samuel is here to stay.'"

I nearly choked on my sandwich. Ethan's hand fell to the table as if he'd forgotten what he'd been doing with it. Jeremy offered Aster a napkin as her meatball came sputtering out of her mouth into her bare hands.

"So it really is him," Stella whispered. "You were right."

"I feel like I missed something here," Jeremy said.

"Where's the Vamguard?" I asked. The Vamguard enforced any discipline the Elder Board felt was needed. Worst case was escorting errant vampires to the Isle where they had to drink animal blood the rest of their lives. This left them barely functionable, always thirsty, and quite mad.

"Locked in the inner sanctum?" Ethan guessed. "They wouldn't leave their post."

Riah's jaw tightened and I realized he had no lunch with him. I'd never seen him go hungry before. I'd never seen him not consume mass amounts of food before. I slid my hand against his forehead to check his temperature. He looked at me funny.

You're skipping lunch?

"I'm freaking out."

Squeezing his hand, I searched my friends' faces. "Could they have sworn themselves to someone else?" They knew more about the lore and function of the abnormal world, no matter what I'd learned in history since I'd been here.

"They aren't wolves, so it's possible." Riah slumped back in his chair, but held tight to my hand.

Jeremy huffed. "Who's Samuel?"

I waved away his question. "Now what?" I asked.

"My dad says Ainsley is heading to the Alpha Court, hoping they'll get involved because of the moon rock. After that, he's going to inform the new elders."

"Ainsley?" Aster echoed. "As in, my dad?"

Riah looked at her. Then at me. I hadn't told her I knew anything about anything. I hadn't told her about the council meeting. He lowered his voice. "They didn't want to alert the new council that anything was up by sending someone who lived in town."

"Will he be back for the full moon?" She held herself very still. Considering she wasn't a very still person, I assumed she must be worried about hunting without him for the first time. I let go of Riah so I could reach across Jeremy and squeeze her fingers.

"*Who* is Samuel?" Jeremy asked again.

"It's a long story."

If Samuel succeeded, what would that look like? And how could we prepare ourselves for what he had planned next when we could hardly wrap our minds around what he had planned for now? We needed a crystal ball.

Then it hit me: *Christian was a crystal ball.*

Nearly knocking my chair over, I charged out to his car, where Aster said he'd been eating lunch since the dance. He was in the backseat, legs hanging out the window.

"Have you dreamt about anything lately?" I asked.

He only looked at me. I opened his passenger door and sat in the front seat, turning to face him. "This is important, Christian. Have you dreamt about anything lately?"

"How important? Life or death important?"

"More important than that. Samuel-taking-over-the-world important."

Oddly, he didn't even react to this, only closed his eyes and breathed heavily on an exhale. "I dream about you. I only ever dream about you now."

I stared at him for a long minute, not knowing how to react to this. He kept his eyes closed, as if he didn't want me to see him or know this.

Of course he didn't. I swallowed hard. "I'm sorry."

"Not your fault." Taking a deep breath, he opened his eyes. They were alarmingly beautiful, and the bright blue sparkling water of them hit me hard. I scanned him, deciding they were more pronounced because the rest of him looked much more lackluster than normal. He'd either not brushed his hair that morning or he'd ran his hand through it a million too many times, which was a nervous tick. It wasn't a tousled, shiny black but fell limp and flat across his forehead. His clothes were wrinkled, and he had dirt under his fingernails.

"Why do you have dirt under your nails?"

"I've been gardening."

"Gardening?"

He wove his hands together on his chest. "It's meditative."

I grinned and he cracked a smile.

"What do you want to know?" he asked.

"Whatever you've got."

"I dreamt Nehemiah and you were caught out of town and locked up. I dreamt Jeremy split your head open with an axe. I dreamt Riah kissed you in the tunnels. And now I'm dreaming that Samuel turns you with the moon rock."

"Turns me?"

Hand through hair. "Into a wolf."

"Are you... Are you so disheveled because you've been worried about me?"

"Getting locked up and split open and turned? Yeah, I'm worried about you." He closed his eyes again. "I hold onto the Riah kissing you part to be what actually comes true. Ironic, right?"

I thought of that moment in the tunnel, me sobbing against Riah for who knows how long. How one of his hands had reached for my waist because it was too narrow to wrap his arms around me, and how that hand had accidentally slipped against skin. Riah reacted like he'd been burned, so much so that I wanted-ed to assure Christian it was the least likely of his dreams to come true. Under the circumstances, though, that seemed cruel.

"Terribly ironic," I agreed.

"I can't help that I dream about you," he said.

I know.

"I didn't think you'd want me to tell you, considering how you seem to be right. I'm trying to learn, Grace. I'm trying to hold my breath and bide my time and wait it out and hope it won't happen."

"Oh, Chris." The agony of that. I could only imagine. But Nehemiah *had* been locked up. And Jeremy had shown me how to throw an axe. Did Christian know that? And if I'd dreamt of Riah and I in that tunnel, I might have thought it was a kiss too.

Which left Samuel, with a moon rock, making his way back to Shady. Because the dreams told truths of Nehemiah and Jeremy and Riah, their connection being me. If Christian's dreams had a homing beacon about them now, it would make sense that Samuel was the next big thing.

I nodded. "Thank you for telling me."

He let out an unsteady breath. "I miss you, Grace."

I blinked at him. "Join us at lunch if you want."

"You and Jeremy?"

"He's just training me."

With a frown, he mumbled, "In the art of kissing?"

"And axe-throwing. But if you can stand to witness it, maybe you can find solace in the fact that your dreams would imply I end up with Riah."

At this, he laughed a little.

"Let me know if any of your dreams change, okay?"

"I'm a little surprised you're buying into it now."

"I'm not going to turn down a crystal ball, whether it's a warning or a riddle or a worry. Right now, we need every clue we can get."

I moved to open the door, but a body flew over the car next to Christian's and landed with a hollow thump against it. I yelped and Christian yanked his legs into the car to sit up.

Reilly shook his shaggy, angular head and crawled over the hood.

Nehemiah appeared and slipped over the car after Reilly, grabbed him by his long hair, and wound up to punch him. I yelled and pounded on the window to get his attention, to get him to stop. He looked crazed, rabid, like he'd mentally gone half wolf. Christian flung his door open as far as it would go, knocking into Nehemiah enough to shake him slightly off focus. It was enough.

Christian stood, the car door between them, his hands up in front of him. Nehemiah looked between us, and I looked between them, and Christian focused on Nehemiah. Right. Thought placement. Chris might be part siren, but he had no more charm than your average charming human. He could, however, place thoughts. Calming thoughts. Logical thoughts. Any thoughts he wanted.

Nehemiah dropped Reilly, who curled over into a ball with a moan, then scrambled on hands and knees away from him, spindly and fast like a spider. Preston ran up and hooked an arm through Reilly's, pulling him even further away.

Nehemiah's chest heaved as he settled his gaze on Christian, until finally he nodded.

"You okay, dude?" Chris asked.

"No. Cleaning up after that bastard got me locked up. I'm very much not okay."

"But you're cool?"

"Cool enough." Nehemiah glanced at me. "Sorry. I..." He swallowed and looked toward his friends, still moving away from him. "Preston, honestly? You're not worried about him drinking you?"

I forced myself to stay steady. To file this information away in a neat pile under a rock that could be overturned and inspected later. The key, I'd found, to handling an abnormal life was to pretend everything you saw and heard was happening in a book, until you had the time and mental focus to dissect it in a safe place.

"Not in the high school parking lot," Preston replied. "And you positively split his face open."

"Better get to the nurse then."

Shady Woods had tilted on its side, and I saw no foreseeable end in sight. If the new elders came in and took care of Samuel, they certainly weren't going to take care of us. That wasn't their thing, protecting abnormals from vampires who acted like vampires. And if the Alpha Court went after Samuel, they wouldn't care about Shady Woods and wolves acting like wolves, either. Not that it even bothered me anymore, them hunting in the area on the full moon.

I wasn't the only one thinking about how Shady was changing, and as I sat down in physics between Jeremy and Stella, Mr. Reinard asked if we thought vampires should be able to hunt in the area since it had been such a successful transition for the wolves.

Jeremy raised his hand. "We hunt people. The wolves are satisfied if they find an animal."

"Why are we having these discussions in physics?" I asked.

"Because physics is what I teach."

"I'm more interested in the convex of magnetism," Stella said.

I glanced at her. That did not at all make sense.

"Oh, I'm definitely interested in the convex of magnetism." Jeremy agreed.

"If you aren't going to take this discussion seriously, I'll send you to the office."

"If you're going to have this discussion, I'd prefer to go to the office," I replied.

"Great." Mr. Reinard crossed his arms. "Do."

I blinked a few times, because who knew it was so easy to get sent to the office?

"What are you waiting for?" he asked.

"Me." Jeremy stood and swept his books off his desk. "She's waiting for me."

I looked back at Stella as we hit the doorway, but she only watched me with wide eyes.

Out in the hall, I asked Jeremy, "What do we do when we get to the office?"

Before he could answer, we turned the corner and ran into Mr. Turner.

"Why aren't you two in class?" he asked, looking between us.

I stammered while telling him what happened, like I might get in trouble for starting such a conversation, but his face went red before I finished, and he marched to Mr. Reinard's room.

Jeremy and I hurried after him.

Mr. Turner stopped hard in the doorway. They'd shuffled around, picking sides since we'd left. "What is this?" he asked.

"A healthy discussion," Mr. Reinard replied.

"Not a physics lesson?"

"Physics is the study of how the fundamental constituents of the universe interact. I would say we are all fundamental constituents of the universe."

"You can't teach them to eat each other."

"I'm not teaching. It's just a discussion."

"If anyone wants to leave," Mr. Turner spoke to the class, "consider yourself excused."

About a third of the students stood up.

"You don't get to excuse my class."

Their conversation, as well as the class, went silent. Mr. Turner must have been saying something in Reinard's head, because Reinard thundered over to shove Turner out of his classroom. Jeremy pulled me out of the way and Turner landed on the floor, skidding across the hall to hit the wall of lockers.

A crowd of students were behind Reinard now, to watch or escape, I couldn't tell. Turner stood, brushing off his vest and khakis, then walked up to Reinard as if the conversation could calmly continue, only to punch Reinard in the face. Reinard charged at Turner again, but stumbled as he swung, giving Turner enough time to step out of the way.

"Careful how much hatred you funnel into me, Jim. Who knows what I might do if I'm overcome by it."

"Is that a threat?"

The class oozed out into the hall to watch our teachers circle each other.

"I don't bother with threats." Reinard's fist made contact with Turner's face. Turner's head whipped over his shoulder in response to the overwhelming power behind that fist, and the subsequent blood spatter hit a few of the students behind him. One of them was a vampire who wiped that blood off his skin with his finger, studied it for a moment, then stuck it in his mouth.

I turned into Jeremy, who put an arm around me.

Turner ducked a fist, landed on his knees, and caught Reinard's calf in a glowing hand. Small white sparks skittered across the floor. Reinard growled in pain.

The principal pushed his way through the crowd to yank Turner up and out of the circle. Mr. Jacobson followed him in and yanked Reinard in the other direction, into his classroom next door.

Mr. Turner and our principal disappeared, their footsteps fading quick, leaving the hall silent and us standing there, an empty space where they'd been. Mr. Reinard didn't come back out of Jacobson's room, and eventually I pushed back into our physics room. The class joined me, little by little, and we sat until the bell rang.

Chapter Fourteen

There for the Taking

Teachers fighting at school over the future of Shady had me feeling so wrong that I was thankful for our scheduled after school run. Sparring wouldn't have felt right, not the way Jeremy liked to mix it with making out, and same with throwing axes. Besides, I didn't think I could control my aim as angry as I was.

Now that the snow had melted and the ground was dry, we started at Riah's, out his backyard onto the trail through the woods. The ground was peppered with a blanket of old needles, dropped last fall, which muffled our steps. Normally it was peaceful, the way the afternoon sun streamed in. Today, however, the shadows felt ominous. As if to warn that these woods were now for hunting.

We ran reasonably fast. As fast as you could run on a thin strip of a trail. Faster than normal, I guessed, because I had to stop and catch my breath, something I didn't do much anymore.

Riah, irritatingly, did not seem out of breath. He didn't seem out of anything. I was working up my energy to give him a nasty look for it when I was distracted by a strange whimpered yelp. Strange in that it sounded alarmingly human.

Ducking into the trees, I wove my way off the path toward the sound, wild growth catching at my feet.

"Grace!" Riah hissed.

We heard it again, along with some hushed voices. I slowed.

Riah's fingertips curled into the fabric of my shirt as he caught up. I leaned back against him, fear unfurling itself from a small point in my stomach. I wasn't sure why, or where it was coming from. There should be nothing scary going on in the middle of the day so close to a residential area. Besides, Riah was with me. Reaching back for his hand, I laced my fingers through his.

Fear or not, I knew we'd both help if someone was in danger.

The whispers quieted, but there was another whimper and the noise of someone dragging something across the forest floor.

As a huge man came into sight, Riah yanked me behind a pine and squeezed me more tightly against him.

Right. We should know what we were getting ourselves into before running into it.

I pegged the man for a wolf, his shoulders wider than any I'd yet seen, and I pegged him for wild. His hair was long and tangled, eyebrows bushy and beard bushier. Bunchy tufts of chest hair pushed out the collar of his shirt and his arm hair was dark and thick. He dragged the thing like it weighed nothing.

I stood on my tiptoes to see what it was and found Mr. Turner. The man was dragging him by the back of his neck, like a dog.

Covering my mouth with my hands, I caught a strangled noise in my throat before it could make it out. Riah rested his forehead against the back of my head, pressure to warn me to be quiet. I did my best to push the horror out of my head, to get control of myself, and sparks fizzled from my fingers.

Good. I might need that. I tried to hold them, tried to keep them.

The wide man reached down and jerked his fingers into one side of Mr. Turner's neck, then his thumb into the other. Blood started dripping from these holes, and the man pulled up, yanking my teacher's throat out.

I made the slightest noise. Ever so slight, but Riah went rigid and the man jerked his head in my direction. He tossed Mr. Turner's body off to the side, like he was baggage and not a sacred life. His throat went next, into the underbrush, and the man licked his hands clean, the whole time staring in our general direction.

The man charged first, but Riah didn't waste any time bursting out of the brush. I'm sure he was trying to make him think it was only him and not me here too, but I quickly gave myself away. I had to see what was happening, had to make sure Riah was okay.

I tested my hands as I watched, the fear I'd felt in Riah's embrace helping an awful lot to get the electricity buzzing through my fingers, and I tried to remember how I'd seen Mr. Turner fight just hours ago.

Gah, Mr. Turner.

The sparks were sharp as they caught inside my clenched fists with nowhere to go, and I sent a burst of sorrow onto the wolf in front of me.

He faltered, giving Riah the edge—Riah, so not built like a stereotypical wolf, not in comparison to this one. Did that mean he wasn't as strong?

They were wrestling and punching—grappling, really—a rough mess like no fight I'd seen before. Not that I'd seen a lot of fights. But this one was frantic. Arms on top of arms, climbing over each other, catching whatever could be caught.

I sent confusion into the man, my brain to his, and he stumbled again, allowing Riah to get the upper hand for a split second. Then he was free, shaking Riah off physically and me off mentally.

As I kept coming with the emotions, trying different ones to see which hit harder, which slowed him down, I stepped closer and closer, out from where I'd been hiding. And as I stepped closer, I felt my hands loosen, my arms relax, my palms turn out.

Not like the fight was over, but like I was readying to be part of it.

Joy almost did it in the end, but it was love that won out. Only the tenth or eleventh emotion I tried, but I guess it made sense. Love was longer-lasting and drew up on everything you loved too. It was hard to fight when you were overwhelmed with love.

Was that crummy of me? Unfair? Did it matter when he'd just ripped my teacher's throat out and would surely do the same to us?

Love and the desire to flee. That was tricky, emotion and thought placement at once. I wasn't sure it actually worked, or if he just didn't want to fight us both when I was toying with his mind enough to level the playing field. Regardless, when he caught sight of me, white sparks spitting out from my palms to hit the dirt at his feet, he scrambled away from Riah and took off at a run, seemingly away from town.

I could not look at Mr. Turner, crumpled behind us.

This hadn't happened.

This couldn't have happened.

When I finally found enough courage to look at Riah, tears sprung to my eyes. For a moment, I was sure I was going to vomit.

Riah wrapped me up in his arms, tight and never-ending, his breath heaving in my hair. "It's okay, you're safe," he muttered, voice as shaky as I felt.

We stood like that for what felt like an hour, clinging to each other.

Will you cover him with something? I finally asked.

Letting go of me, I retraced our steps, leaving him to do it on his own. I felt mildly guilty about this, but the further I got, the more I needed to get out. The more I imagined the wolf coming back for me, alone, and I ran.

Riah caught up to me as I neared his yard, and we broke out of the trees together.

My head was pounding, and my arms and cheek hurt from running blindly through branches as the tears blurred my vision. Riah had a gash down the side of his face. His shirt was torn, one side of his chest exposed, revealing a patchwork of what would soon enough be bruises.

My hurt was mostly shock and anger, but his was physical pain.

His parents weren't home, his sisters either. We walked through the house and I grabbed my keys. I could do this, no matter how badly I was shaking. I could drive him to the clinic and get him seen by Dr. Riley. It was only a few blocks. I could keep it together for just a few blocks.

Riah asked me a few questions on the way but I didn't an-swer, too focused on my shaking hands and my shaking insides and trying not to vomit as we made our way through town. I screeched to a stop around the back of the clinic and helped Riah out of the car, then through the employee door.

Chris? I called. *Are you here?*

Where's here? he replied.

The clinic.

Next door. Blood bank. What's going on?

We need siren tears. I settled Riah onto the large trash can in the supply room, then slipped down the hall to another open door where Mr. Riley's two nurses shared a workspace. I did not want to go out to reception. I did not want to see more people than necessary. I just wanted siren tears.

No nurses, but fresh tears, there for the taking. I had worked here. I'd done this before. I only felt mildly bad leaving a note and taking one of the smaller jars back for Riah.

Handing him the glass to hold, I dipped my finger into the silver and let it sit a moment while it gathered itself together, searching for somewhere to go and something to do, as if it was collectively a sentient being shed from another sentient being. When I felt its pulse more strongly than my own, I lifted my finger to the gash on his cheek. He winced.

It hurts? I asked.

He lifted a shoulder haphazardly. "It moves, gets in there, wiggles around, you know."

I did know. I'd just never had as deep of a wound as this one. I held my finger there until the tears filled in the gash the way tar would fill in a crack, then moved to a few other superficial cuts on his face.

My finger was stuck on his lip—my gaze too—when the back door slammed open, startling both of us. My hand shot down to catch the jar, but Riah had it stable and I only caught his hand instead.

"What happened?" Christian asked from the hall as he spotted us in the tiny closet.

I shook my head, trying to speak, to explain that I was okay, that it was just my brain that was scrambled from what I'd seen out there, but words made me feel like I couldn't breathe.

Christian turned me to him, pushing my tangled hair out of my face and checking me over.

I wiped at my tears but couldn't rid myself of the image of Mr. Turner's throat.

Riah rested a few knuckles into the jar of siren tears, and I brushed my fingers off on my joggers. They glowed there like a firefly, incandescent, brilliant and yet fading.

Riah was a wolf too, I reminded myself. They weren't all the type to rip throats out. Aster, too. Kiara. I looked directly at Christian and tried to draw myself up with some authority. "I'm okay."

"No," Riah corrected. "You are most certainly not okay."

"I am. I'm okay." I had to be. I had to have the strength it took to live in this town.

"I've been asking you questions for ten minutes and you haven't heard a thing. You're in shock."

"I'm not in shock."

His lip was no longer busted but still a little puffy, and I held my hand out for his. Silver siren tears clinging to his knuckles, he took my fingers. "I'm okay," I said again. "It's Mr. Turner who's not okay. He's in the woods by your house."

That was when I noticed Dr. Riley behind Christian. "Could you bring me to him?" he asked.

I shook my head. "It's too late."

The silence that fell was so complete I could hear the animals in the basement, scurrying around in their cages. The animals kept for their blood, to treat and heal vampires. But why? Why not let them find their own, if they're out hunting anyway.

Dr. Riley broke the silence by muttering something about us staying there and him calling the police.

Christian shook his head. "I don't understand. I didn't dream this."

"Good." I couldn't imagine what that would have been like.

"No! Not good!" He seemed angry, and Riah gave him a warning look.

"It means you aren't as into me," I muttered.

Christian squinted his eyes in confusion. "How am I supposed to protect you if I don't know what you're up against?"

"What *we're* up against," I corrected. It was collective, this thing that suddenly loomed, that before had felt like strange little problems, one-offs that could be swept under the rug or worried about later, things that couldn't get too bad because Shady had been Shady for a few hundred years. But now. Well, we'd missed the bigger picture and now that's all I could see, the bigger picture looming over us. "And it's not your job to protect me."

"But I *am* as into you," Christian muttered. "I don't get it."

There was no use arguing with him. I turned back to Riah and checked his hands, ran my fingers through his hair, found a little blood, moved a little siren tear.

What about your torso? I asked, trailing a gaze down his chest. I cleared my throat. *Anywhere else hurt?*

His eyes were on mine as I brought them back up to his face.

I don't know why it felt so intimate. We'd swam together in Stella's backyard multiple times and my ex-boyfriend was standing behind me. Yet as Riah watched me and I watched him it felt like we were the only two people there.

"Need me to get more tears?" Chris asked in a small voice. "Those will all be bruises if we don't do something about it."

"I can live with bruises," Riah said, his attention not wavering from me. "It's just my rib here that particularly hurts."

"Sure," I said. "Yes, more tears." Then I took the jar from him and scraped out the final bits to rest them on the spot he was talking about as gently as I could.

Goose bumps spread over his skin.

"Are you cold?"

"No."

Shortly after Christian came back and took over the nursing, Officer Andres knocked and stepped in the back door. She, at least, was old Shady. Good Shady.

She was also a siren and was leading with charm. I sighed into it. Siren charm sometimes felt like relief.

Before she could say anything, I closed my eyes and brought the memory up to the forefront, then pushed it out at her.

When I opened my eyes, the look of compassion on her face nearly gutted me. "I'm sorry you had to see that."

She took a few notes, asked Riah a few questions, radioed to someone where Mr. Turner's body was, then slipped out as gracefully as she'd slipped in. Dr. Riley came back and gave us both a more complete exam, checking Riah's ribs and handing him some vampire blood to speed the healing of anything internal that the tears couldn't reach. He told us to let him know if we still hurt tomorrow or the next day, then cleared us to go. Christian walked out with us, through the back door the way we'd come.

"Where are you taking her?" Christian asked Riah.

"I'm taking him home," I replied, my voice steely. Riah had been through exactly what I'd been through, only he'd been more battered and bruised than me.

Christian ran his hand through his hair and pulled at the ends a little. "Will you call me later so I know you're okay?"

"I'm okay," I assured, as Riah and I opened car doors simultaneously and slid into our seats.

Christian kneeled next to me and reached for my hand, a warm blue fuzz emanating off his fingers. I responded in kind, now that I seemed to have control over it, and we stared at the electricity bouncing back and forth between our fingers.

Standing to press a warm—but no longer stinging—hand against my cheek, Christian nodded at Riah, then headed across the street back to the blood bank.

Chapter Fifteen

I Can't

"Is this what's going to happen when we don't agree now?" I whispered to Riah once we were safe in his bedroom. "We'll rip each other's throats out?"

"You think this had to do with him and Reinard today?"

I shrugged. What else could it be about? "Do we have to hide that we're pacifists?"

"It's not something to hide. Just maybe not something to argue about."

He was standing in front of his open window, the chill March air sweeping in and blowing his hair every so often. I was draped across the foot of his bed, face down because that felt appropriate.

We stopped talking because it was too chilling to talk about, and before I knew it, the window was dark, Riah was gone, and a blanket had been tossed over me.

Amazing that I'd drifted off to sleep. You'd think that after watching an innocent man's throat get ripped out, normal things wouldn't work the same. Like sleep, how days and nights worked, or how the sun set.

My text messages told me Riah was at Ethan's, and that Aster's dad reached the Alpha Court. They were "...irate with the blatant disregard... manipulation that is the rock..." and they would "...not stand for being manhandled by a vampire as if wolves were some common pet..."

They were hoping to lure Samuel to Shady, a safer place than most to confront him, and Riah wasted no time in going to talk to Ethan's mom. Violet and Samuel obviously had a connection, hopefully the kind that would bring Samuel here if she requested it. If nothing else, Riah was convinced she could get word to him. He hadn't wanted to wake me.

I hurried down the stairs smelling of Riah and his bed. Awkwardly, my mom met me at the bottom of the stairs with a sandwich. She folded me into her arms like she did when I was little. I let her kiss my forehead and hold me tight.

"Riah's mom called me," she muttered. "Are you okay?"

"I'm going to find Riah," I explained. He now felt like an appendage I couldn't be without. Honestly, maybe he always had, but now there was a more urgent tug. The utter panic of how Riah could have ended up like Mr. Turner still thrummed in my chest.

Even though it turned my stomach, I bit into the sandwich to convince her I was all right. The slice of tomato between my teeth felt like flesh, bringing back to mind a bloody, discarded throat, and I had to force myself not to visibly recoil. I figured the basic act of chewing and swallowing and being hungry would prove to her that I was functioning and capable of leaving on my own to find Riah.

"Okay," she said. "But we need to talk later."

I nodded.

"Soon." She eyed the sandwich, so I took another bite. As I moved for the front door, she went back to the kitchen.

Hurrying outside, I spit the tomato into the bushes.

They weren't in the basement for once, but sitting around the kitchen table: Ethan, Riah, and Violet.

Steff, the current Mrs. Parrino, stood by the empty chair with Ethan's little sister on her hip. She smiled at me and headed up the stairs. Mr. Parrino was leaning against the counter. I slid over to settle next to him, not wanting to take Steff's seat if she were coming back, and also certain I didn't want to be a part of the conversation.

It had started raining on my way over, and I was self-conscious that I was dripping on Mr. Parrino's floor. He was the scariest person in this town, if you asked me. Or he had been, and I was still holding onto that for a little bit. Because as intimidating as he was, I knew he wouldn't hurt anyone. At least, not unless he had to. My dad had been in that position, a few times.

"Samuel could not have meant for this," Riah was saying. So I'd missed the small talk.

"A few humans from neighboring towns are unavoidable in the changeover," Violet said, speaking of the bodies drained. "You have to give most wilds a little time to curtail their instincts. They can make the choice and still fall back into it. They can want this life and still be called to hunt. It will get better."

"That doesn't explain the dendrite and the throat." I was impressed how firm Riah's tone was when he said this. Mine would have been high and shaky if I had to talk about it.

She shifted in her seat.

"Samuel esteems dendrites," Ethan reminded. Her words.

She glanced over at me, and Mr. Parrino spoke. "Don't you think he'd want to know about this?"

We all looked at him. He said it as if he knew Samuel too. I supposed, if Samuel had been the one to take her away...

"Listen, Mom, I've met him a few times." Ethan shifted in his seat. "I don't trust him, but I trust that he wouldn't want abnormals of any kind turning on each other."

"You have to tell him," Riah pushed. "He has to come talk to the wilds here. If this is what he wants for the world, he needs to make sure it's starting right. If we turn on each other, that's not going to bode well for a new world order. He needs this to be an example of what could be, in a way that no abnormal could argue against. He needs to be able to hold out his hand and say, see here, this is what we're aiming for."

"He's right," Mr. Parrino said. He looked at his ex-wife evenly, as if she hadn't let him down, as if she wasn't now living in his house again with ideals vastly different from his own.

In good news, she hadn't said she didn't know how to get a hold of Samuel, which implied she did.

The heavy rain gave way to thunder, shaking the house with a violent clap. The branches of the hydrangea outside the kitchen window slammed against it so hard I thought the glass might crack.

Violet ran a hand through her curly black hair, tugging it once halfway through, then pushed back from the table and stood. "Fine. I guess this is why he gave me a phone in the first place."

She reached a hand out to Mr. Parrino as she passed, and he took it for a moment. Then she was gone, up the stairs to where she was sleeping on the floor of Ethan's little sister's room.

Ethan said they were best friends now. Petal left her stuffed animals on Violet's sleeping bag, sharing them with her, a new one every night. He said he could hear his mom telling Petal bedtime stories from his room, and that once he'd snuck his head in to find them holding hands, that his mom had slid her sleeping bag all the way over next to Petal's little toddler bed. Eric couldn't stand it, the stories or his mother's murmuring, because it brought them both right back to when they were that age. When she was still there.

Mr. Parrino was staring at me.

"Yes, sir?"

"I want you to know it was unconscionable, what you saw. It shouldn't have happened here or anywhere. Normal or abnormal, that was a murder and nothing else."

I swallowed hard, fighting the tears.

He put a thin hand on my shoulder and looked me straight in the eye. "It doesn't matter the reason it happened. Wilds might kill for food but they do not murder. Do not let what you saw color anything differently about the people you know and the town we've built here. That was the same as a stabbing in a back alley, understand?"

I nodded, because that's what you did when Mr. Parrino asked if you understood something, even if you didn't exactly.

Was he trying to tell me Shady was no more dangerous than Chicago?

Then he was gone too, up the stairs to one or both of his wives, and Ethan and Riah were staring at me. Ethan was close to perfecting his dad's look, and Riah wore so much on his face I could hardly breathe.

So much I couldn't read, and something I couldn't quite put my finger on.

"I should get home," he said. "My mom didn't want me gone too long."

Ethan stood up and wrapped me in a hug, his long arms like straps around me. Then he clasped Riah on the shoulder and headed up the stairs himself.

We were family; we let ourselves in and out.

Riah and I made our way to the front door. The rain was pelting down in such force that everything outside was a blur.

"You're not walking home in this." It was somewhere between a question and a statement.

Silence, but for the pelting and clapping and booming outside.

He stepped past me onto the porch and I followed him out. We were squeezed together, barely shielded by the house's meager overhang. At least the rain was pouring sideways, away from us.

"Take my car. Bring it back in the morning."

"I can walk, Grace. I'm not afraid of a little thunder."

"Riah, we just watched someone's throat get ripped out. I don't care if you're the biggest, baddest wolf. I need to know you're safe in my car. Then you bring it right back in the morning, because I don't want to be without you right now."

"You don't want to be without me?"

Maybe it was the twisted night, all that had happened that day, or the energy of the storm that filled the space between us, but we'd been this close a million times before, closer even, and it had never felt quite like this.

"Can't," I corrected, looking away. "I can't be without you."

He opened his mouth. Then closed it.

I handed him my keys, then ran across Ethan's front lawn, across my driveway to my porch. When I reached it, I turned back. Riah still stood under the porch light, watching me, but my mom was opening our front door, ready for another bottom-of-the-stairs talk as I'd come to think of them. The big things that can't wait until you sit down around a table or get a glass of water. The big things that can't be said on the phone or via text.

I had a sneaking suspicion I knew which one of those big things we were going to be revisiting.

Sure enough, as soon as I took the door from her, she turned and sat on the bottom of the stairs at the other end of the small entryway. I slumped down next to her and we sat for a moment in the tumultuous quiet. Tumultuous because the wind was howling, the rain beating down, and the branches scraping wherever they could reach.

"Your dad and I are thinking that after Justin and Clara get married, we'll sell them the house and move to Madison." Her voice was gentle, but I could tell it wasn't meant to be a discussion.

Justin and Clara were getting married that summer, a few months before I turned eighteen. If I was eighteen, my parents couldn't keep me, right? Surely my grandparents or my brother would let me live with them for my senior year.

"You'd come with us," she said.

I shot a look at her. "I didn't say anything."

"You slipped." She tapped her head.

"Perfect. Guess we can't go back to normal then, in case I do it again."

"You let your guard down with loved ones sometimes. The veil can get hazy and more permeable. We can move back. You know plenty."

"I can't believe you're going to move me somewhere strange all over again. You think it was easy hiding myself in Chicago? You think it wouldn't be ten times harder to hide now, after the way you've let me live for the last three years?"

"Honey, you've been through too much. Your dad and I can't put you through any more of this, and things in town don't seem to be getting better." She sighed. "If I'd known it wouldn't be the same experience for you that it was for me so many years ago, we never would have come back."

"I cannot leave these people. The day I turn eighteen, I'm coming back." The thought of leaving Riah in particular made me very, very distraught.

"I know you'll miss your friends, but they can visit."

"They can't visit!" I wailed. "How can they visit?!"

"Our home would be a safe place for them. We can find blood somewhere for Ethan and can provide enough water for Stella. Riah and Aster would be easy. They'll visit."

"They won't visit! They'll turn out like Charlie and Mateo who hardly know me anymore. I hardly talk to them. Then I'll have to start all over in college, one more time. Yeah, you know what? Fine. Take me. Then instead of college, I'll just come back here."

"Grace, you're going to college."

"That's what you told Justin. Dr. Riley would snap me up in a minute as an intern or a nurse. Done. I'm set."

She took my chin and made me look at her. "You're going to college."

I jerked away and stood up. "How can you turn your back on all of this? This is who we are! It's like you're abandoning your own people."

She huffed a little. "Sometimes you have to put your children first. I know you can't understand that yet, but what I need is to keep you safe. And I haven't been doing a very good job of that since we moved here. I can't fail again."

"You haven't failed!" I cried. "You've given me everything I didn't know I needed! There's no doubt this is where I'm supposed to be."

She stood up to tuck a piece of hair behind my ear. It was something she did when she was worried about me—futzed with my appearance to have her hands on me, when a hug would only make her worry more obvious.

"If you want to put me first, then you'll keep us here. You'll keep us here and you won't abandon Justin. Is dad really okay leaving Justin behind?"

She slumped back down on the stairs.

"Yeah. He's not coming with," I reminded. "He's marrying a vampire."

As the storm smashed against the front door and the electricity flickered out, she looked up at me. "Please, bunny."

"No. I will not make this easy for you." And I swept up to my room before the tears burst out of me. I couldn't stop them at this point, but she couldn't see them or she'd hug me and we'd fold in together like origami that couldn't be pulled back apart. Then, before I knew it, I'd be in Madison starting a depressing and constricting senior year where I couldn't breathe for the distance from Riah and the rest of my people. From home.

My mom was at my door before I could close it.

"What if things tank here?" she asked. "What if the elitists or purists or wilds turn on us and we need to flee? Then what?"

The hope I extracted from that soothed me, helped my lungs start working again. "Then I'd want to flee with the others, or make a new town, or figure out how to fight against them. You do realize Samuel is working on a grand scale here, and if he succeeds, we're just humans in Madison."

"Someone needs to protect the humans."

"That's not putting me first. That's not putting Justin or Grandma or Grandpa or our people first. That's putting innocents first, innocents who might not even accept us. If it's us or them, then we're the them. So don't give me this crap about putting me first. You're putting your fear first."

We stared at each other in the lightning-laced dark. And I swore to myself that I, for one, was done putting my fear first.

Chapter Sixteen

A Bloody Hoard

Mr. Turner had disappeared walking home from class. He lived in Riah's neighborhood and his wife called the school. After hearing what had happened earlier that day, she blamed Mr. Reinard, but there was no proof he had any connection to the wolf who'd dragged him into the forest and ripped his throat out.

We had memorial assemblies for him that first week after he passed, every morning until his funeral, and I suddenly couldn't stop worrying about everyone when I didn't have eyes on them. As sure as I was that I wanted to stay in Shady, I knew what real anxiety was now. I woke up with it every morning, and it didn't ease until I was able to verify that all my people were in one piece.

As Ethan and I walked into school the first morning we didn't have an assembly, I stood on my tiptoes and craned my neck like an idiot, only spotting Aster and Jeremy.

Jeremy was a little testy with me, in the coolest vampire kind of way, because I'd stood him up the last too many days. He thought

I should jump back into sparring and axe-throwing and kissing and running, but I just wanted to sit in Ethan's basement with Riah, Stella, and Ethan and remember how innocent Shady had been when I first arrived.

Stella was waiting at Ethan's locker. She reached out to squeeze my hand as I walked past, offering a burst of charm with her touch.

I made it to my locker but neither Riah nor his sisters were there yet. Though the hallway was swarming, there was no sign of them.

I had no reason to think anything had happened. None. Slamming my locker shut, I tried to ignore what their absence was doing to my chest. I pounded my sternum with my fingertips, willing the pain to subside, and called out for Christian.

I'm here.

Yes, it was awkward checking on your ex who wasn't exactly over you, but I also found I couldn't not.

I closed my eyes and leaned my head back against the cool metal, waiting, listening for their voices, any of them, but mostly Riah's. I sorted through the rest of the students in the hall for his laugh, his chuckle, his tone.

Where *were* they? They were killing me here.

My eyes snapped open as I heard Ava. She and Maribel were digging in their lockers. But where was Riah? I could've screamed.

"You desperately need to calm down," he said from the other side of me.

"Don't ever do that again." I smacked him. "Where were you?"

He motioned in Ava's direction. "Outfit crisis."

I cocked my head. She was in jeans and a tight black tee. Maribel, on the other hand, was in a flowing patchwork maxi skirt and an untucked black men's button down, her dark hair about to her waist and pinned back with five green bobby pins. She had jelly bracelets up one arm and an octopus on her bare wrist that Riah probably drew while they waited for Ava to decide on her outfit. "You could have texted me."

"My every move?" He grinned. "Are you worried about me?"

"Of course I'm worried about you," I snapped. "Aren't you worried about me?"

His smile fell. "Yes, but that's how it's always been. I worry about you and you carry on with your life as if you're invincible."

I was the worst about needing proximity to my people, but they were as worried—if not more worried—about me, considering it had been Riah and I in those woods, seeing what we saw, fighting who we fought.

In Spanish first hour, Aster scooted her desk all the way next to mine. We faced the windows and the front of the school, and I lost track of time as I watched a group of five wilds milling in the street. I remember thinking how I'd never get used to the sight of them, but now, somehow, it hardly registered. Like leaves that slowly drop in the fall, you don't really think much about it until one day they're all there, on the ground beneath your feet. Until one day, one of them kills your teacher.

In trig, Aster did the desk thing again and Stella set up some sort of ambient charm cloud that felt like relaxing in a mental spa space for the hour.

In English, we had tables which were currently set in a circle for better discussion of what we were reading. Riah normally sat between Ethan and I, but they moved so I now sat between them.

And so it went.

As rough as every morning was, that night was the full moon, which was even worse. Being separated from Riah had definitely become more difficult, and I was up late texting Jeremy, telling him I wasn't in a good place for a relationship. He replied that we could call it whatever I wanted and keep kissing. Did I not want to kiss him anymore?

I'd fallen asleep to that, because it took me a minute to decide if I did or not, and it was late enough that a minute was all it took for me to fall asleep.

I woke at the crack of dawn to whispers and footsteps in the house, my phone still in my hand. Panic shot through my limbs at what kind of news would come so early in the morning, and I tore down the steps to find out what was wrong.

Instead of police telling my parents that something terrible had happened to Riah, I found a hoard of men. Huge, hulking bloody men with chest hair sprouting like thick forests out the collars of their shirts and beards clotted with dried blood. Were-wolves.

My dad was smiling in welcome and Mr. Jenkins was there. Riah appeared in front of where I stood on the bottom step. How he made it through the thick pack in the small foyer, I didn't know, but I threw my arms around him and held on tight.

His lips accidentally brushed my neck. I visibly shivered and my hands fizzed.

"You all right?" he whispered.

"I am now." *Why did you bring all these wolves to my house and why are they bloody and you're not?*

"I swim after. Some don't." He pulled away from me, leaving an aching, cold emptiness in his wake. "The Alpha Court apparently doesn't."

My eyes widened a bit on the hulking masses before me. *Why is the Alpha Court at my house?*

"They're going to hide out here and wait for Samuel. They figure he'll show up to see Violet before doing anything else."

My mom appeared in the archway between the foyer and the kitchen with four mugs of coffee in her hands. They were snatched up and she retreated for more, the mass following her and leaving the small entry empty, only Riah in front of me.

I studied him for any bruising or cuts, lifting up his shirt to check his chest and making him turn so I could see his back as well. When I eyed the waistband of his pants, he raised an eyebrow and snorted. "I'm fine. I promise."

My phone buzzed in my hand, pulling at our attention. Jeremy.

"He call you every morning?" Riah asked.

"No, that's weird." Except I'd fallen asleep before answering him about whether or not I wanted to kiss him anymore. I bit my lip. Then shook my head and silenced it. I didn't want to talk to Riah about who I was or wasn't kissing. I didn't know when or why that had changed, but it had. "So, we have houseguests?"

"They'll be staying in the basement."

"After they wash themselves."

He laughed a little. "After they wash themselves."

"Grace?" My mom appeared in the archway again. "Go get eight towels please, and then get ready for school."

Chapter Seventeen

Five Pieces of Him

It took some getting used to, the smell in the house.

Sort of like a men's locker room. Not that I'd been in a men's locker room, but I'd definitely smelled the boys as they came off gym or a basketball game, and this was that, only magnified.

Riah was drawn to them, wanting to have a snack at our house after school, or asking if he could come for dinner, even though they ate in the basement and he was too intimidated to join them.

Jeremy was still training me, sparring with me and throwing axes, but we hadn't kissed since that text I'd never replied to. I hadn't left him hanging on purpose, but I'd been distracted for too long and then it seemed awkward to say anything about it. Besides, I wasn't exactly sure what the answer was. He stayed at our table but spent more time with Aster now than anyone else. Which meant Aster spent less time with us and it was sort of back to us four at Ethan's. Waiting on Samuel. Wondering when he'd show up. If he'd show up.

And then he did.

Ethan led us into his kitchen after school just like any other day and there Samuel sat, at the table with Violet, grins on their faces like he'd just arrived, fingers linked on the table as they caught up.

When Violet noticed Ethan, how he'd stopped in the doorway, bracing himself with hands on either side of the doorframe, she let go of Samuel's hand and wiped it on her pants.

Mom. No doubt she could hear me only a house away. *He's here. In the kitchen.*

"Ethan, have you met Samuel?" Violet asked, soft and tentative.

"Unfortunately."

"Now, son, don't be like that." Samuel stood, looking every bit as arrogant as he ever had, plus some, which is how I realized it had been arrogance all along. He took measured steps to Ethan with his hand out. "Let's start over, for your mom's sake."

"I don't owe my mom anything."

"Please don't be difficult." Violet crossed her hands on the table. "He's here, isn't he? A show of faith."

"You should be proud," Samuel said to Ethan, glancing back at Violet before tucking his hand against his side, unshaken. "Your mother has built quite a community here. Now if we can just merge her community and yours a little more seamlessly, we'll be all set."

"All set for what?" Riah asked.

We were grouped in the doorway. Ethan first, Stella looking over his right shoulder, me looking over his left, and Riah with his hands on my waist looking over mine.

The back door opened, and one of the Alpha Court stepped in, filling the space. Samuel turned, as slowly as I'd ever seen a vampire move.

"Do you have it?" the werewolf asked.

Samuel took a step back and scanned the room. "Of course I have it."

I raised an eyebrow. If we were talking about what I thought we were talking about, he'd definitely lost it once. Good to see he hadn't left it in anyone else's hands.

Where are you? my mom asked.

Next door? Because where else would she think I was?

Grace! Get out of there!

Glancing back at Riah, about to tell my friends we'd forgotten that part of the plan, I saw another court member at the front door. At this point, our best bet to extricate ourselves was to head up or down the stairs.

"Hand it over."

"You'll have to tear me apart to get it."

"If you don't hand it over, we *will* tear you apart."

Violet was up in a vampire instant, standing between Samuel and the wolf. But Samuel only smiled, as if even this had been part of his plan. Or he'd make it part of his plan.

"Martyrs rise to greatness in a way the living cannot." He held his arms out to his sides, as if he were offering himself up, then shoved through the basement door vampire fast.

The tunnels.

The tunnels.

Violet went after him.

Mom! The tunnels!

The wolves at both doors didn't move.

There are vampires coming from Parrino's to block his way. Come home. Now.

Stumbling past Riah, I moved to the front door and looked up at the mountain of a wolf-man who literally filled the entire space. He stepped aside just enough to let me pass, and I walked out to a front lawn and three wolves.

Three actual in-form wolves. Huge wolves. *Holy crap*. They were insanely beautiful, but huge. Three times the size of a normal wolf. Definitely bigger than the one who'd been in our kitchen last year.

I backed away from them, though they didn't seem crazed, then ran once I hit our driveway. The door was open, my mom waiting for me. She caught me in her arms, grabbing for Riah too, holding onto him with one hand while she hugged me, then pulling Stella in with her other as she reached arm's length. Ethan shut the door and sunk to the floor.

Before long, we heard a screech outside. Ethan shot over to the window. Stella wrapped her arms around him from behind and watched for a minute over his shoulder, then buried her face in his back. Riah joined them. I left my mom to see what was happening.

Samuel's arm had been torn off and tossed to one of the wolves. The wolf caught it with his teeth, took a careful but solid bite, then dropped it in the grass next to him.

"They're not out of their mind," I muttered.

"They're Court." My mom put a hand on my shoulder. "They're never out of their mind."

"To become an Alpha, they have to tear the moon rock out of the one before them and swallow it," Riah muttered. "They only live if they're worthy, and if they live, they've mastered their instinct."

The ache in his voice, wanting that control so desperately, had me about to kiss him on the cheek. Samuel let out another shriek, pulling my attention back outside as the wolf bit into Samuel's second loose arm. It wasn't nearly as gory as watching a human be dismembered, since vampire blood didn't bleed the same as human blood, but it made me sick just the same.

"I don't suppose I can convince you all to step away from the window?" my mom asked.

Ethan and Riah shook their heads, and Stella was buried in Ethan's back anyway.

"Grace?"

I shook my head too but stepped closer to Riah, behind him, so I couldn't see the worst of it for the sake of my somersaulting stomach.

Violet stepped out the front door, Mr. Parrino and Steff spilling out behind her as if they'd been trying to detain her but had lost their grip. They caught her again on the porch when she took in the scene in front of her, and she folded in their arms, letting out a long, tortured wail.

I stopped watching when it looked like the two court members were about to rip one of Samuel's legs off.

"That won't kill him," Riah muttered. "Why are they giving him a second chance?"

I gaped at my mother. "Pulling him apart is giving him a second chance?"

"It's giving them time," she clarified. "It gives them until the next full moon. If he's put back together by then, he'll turn into a wolf. If he isn't, when he turns, when those pieces become wolf and no longer vampire, he'll bleed out."

"Time to what?" I asked.

"Samuel is a vampire, under the Elder's jurisdiction. It gives them time to make sure the Elder Board is okay with them destroying him."

When we turned back to Ethan's front yard, Violet's screaming had stopped. She was a limp ragdoll in her ex-husband's arms, sobbing like I couldn't imagine a vampire to ever sob, and all eight of the Alpha Court were in human form again. Duct tape had been wrapped around Samuel's head to cover his mouth, and they carried the five pieces of him down the street, past our house.

Chapter Eighteen

If It Takes

The Alpha Court walked the center of the road, all the way to town hall.

Word was that they didn't even bother moving for cars. They strutted into the building with Samuel's dismembered, bitten body parts under their arms and asked to see Ron Ashby or Sean Jenkins.

They were directed into Ron's office, and Ron called Riah's dad in. They hadn't wanted to leave without thanking them for the letter and assuring them that they would take care of Samuel one way or another.

Once they were gone, the rest of the council members called a meeting. They wanted to know why Ron and Sean had sent the Court after Samuel, why they'd do such a thing without talking to them first.

They hadn't realized it was a town problem, Ron explained, and didn't want to take up valuable manpower when it had nothing to do with Shady Woods.

The council asked what they were supposed to do with the wilds in town now.

Riah's dad suggested that the previous councils had done a pretty good job making decisions on their own, based on what was best for the town. He reminded them that this was what they'd vowed to do when inducted into office, and insisted that no council he was on would take orders from any puppeteer, no matter how smart said puppeteer might seem.

They fired him.

"But they can't fire a council member," I said for the umpteenth time as we drove out to Aster's after school. It was the first time Riah had told the story to her, Christian, and Jeremy.

We were headed there because Samuel had been pulled apart in Ethan's front lawn and my house still smelled like a locker room. Thank goodness it was almost May. We had every window open to air the place out.

"Well, they did," Riah replied, for the umpteenth time. For Aster, Jeremy, and Christian's benefit, he added, "Now Ron Ashby's the only one with any sense."

"That has to be illegal or something," Aster said. "Elected officials have to be fired by the people, not by their peers."

"They aren't abiding by any particular laws or traditions, so I'm not sure why you think this would be any different."

Aster's mom's shiny sedan was parked in the garage next to her brother's kit car. In the drive was Aster's dad's ancient, rounded truck in mint condition. It was also mint-colored, which was not what I would have expected from a reclusive werewolf who'd lost many children, never got over it, and left his wife for the wilderness.

The house was an old farmhouse with multiple off-shoots and additions. A room here and a room there, a screened porch and a greenhouse. A sunroom wall-papered with dragonflies that looked like it had been meant for a play room but was her mom's office. Adelaide Stickman edited the paper, wrote for the paper, and also conducted interviews on the radio program when it aired, which seemed to happen more and more frequently these days.

Somehow, all the extra, empty, pastel-colored rooms in the house were not sad, but rather like a photograph of a wistful memory. They'd been built for all the babies expected and lost, which was probably another reason Aster's dad couldn't live here anymore and why her mom couldn't leave.

We found all three of them in the sunroom, where Aster's mom sat in her office chair facing the room and her dad sat on the ledge of the window. Adam was leaning in the doorway and they were giving him a hard time about a recent test grade, being mostly jovial about it, laughing and looking at each other in a way that implied they might get back together any moment. Maybe this was how they always were, though I had no idea when they'd last seen each other. The way Aster made it sound, her dad only left his cabin in the woods for the full moon, and her mother only sent her and her brother with provisions, never visiting herself.

Ainsley stood as we entered. Towering over all of us, he cooed over how big Jeremy and Christian had gotten since he'd seen them last, when, he said, they'd only been up to his knees.

Adam pushed himself off the doorframe to flick Aster's ear, to which she cupped the back of his head as he snuck out of the room.

Her mom stood from her desk and moved to follow Adam. "I'll get some snacks."

"Any word on the Elders?" Aster asked her dad.

"They're in place. They contacted the higher captains of the Vamguard. Those who'd been assigned to the control center are missing, but no one else had gotten wind of anything."

So Samuel's reach hadn't stretched that far at least. He had no army.

"Power hungry S.O.B," Jeremy muttered.

I looked over at him. "Violet said that's not what it's about."

"She said he's making up for everything, for everyone he's lost, so we—collectively—will never be lost again." Riah rolled his eyes.

Violet had been kind of hysterical the last few days. Another reason we were avoiding Ethan's. Between Riah and I, we thought it kind of odd they were still letting her stay there.

"What happened to the moon rock?" Christian asked.

Ainsley cleared his throat, waited until all five of us turned our attention to him, then tapped his sternum. "They asked me to take it on. I'm here for goodbyes."

It took us all a minute for his words to make any sense, but what he was saying was that there was a new Court member.

Aster blinked at him. Then blinked some more in an attempt to thwart her tears. He didn't mean a goodbye until the next full moon. There were no more full moons for him, only duty. The Alpha Court couldn't have a family. They couldn't have attachments. They could only have the pack.

"There will be nine of you now?"

"There are."

Aster let out a little yelp and threw her arms around his waist.

If this is a goodbye, we should probably leave, Christian said to Riah, Jeremy, and me.

Aster was shaking her head, sniffling and muttering. I couldn't seem to leave her, and Riah had to drag me past. Then it was me, Riah, Christian, and Jeremy in my car.

Awkward.

Jeremy was the first to speak. "We could go see a movie." But I was already past the turn.

"Basketball?" Christian asked him. "My house?"

"Sure, man." And they did that stupid handshake thing the basketball team liked to do.

Some things, at least, didn't change.

As I drove them back to school, to their cars, I counted how many wilds roamed the streets. A few had definitely fled back into their wild corners, deciding against mainstreaming in any way, but their numbers still seemed to be growing.

Christian and Jeremy were loud in the backseat, which I noticed more after they got out of the car and slammed the doors shut, leaving Riah and I in their wake.

After they drove off, I rolled my windows down and set my knees up on my steering wheel.

"We could go to my house," Riah offered, but he was getting comfortable too, resting his back against the door so he faced me. His hair lifted up and fluttered in the breeze.

Taking a deep breath of the fresh spring air, I shook my head. "Too many people for right now." His sisters always had friends over.

"How are you doing?" he asked.

I thought of Jeremy's mom. She's how I wanted to be doing. "Hey. Want to help me build some targets in my backyard?"

"Targets?"

"For axe-throwing. Have you ever thrown an axe?"

He shook his head. "What if you miss? That guy behind you mows his lawn constantly. You could take his head off."

"Your backyard then. Or the clearing on the trail."

"That mean you're done with Jeremy?" he asked.

"I mean, we're friends."

"But, the kissing?"

"We haven't kissed in a while. Not that we'd had an official conversation about it. Figure if I can find another place to throw axes, our relationship—or whatever it was—will just fizzle out." I held my palms up and showed him some fizzle.

Biting back a smile, he straightened in his seat. "By all means, then. Let's build something in the clearing."

I nodded and started my car. Building something felt like doing something. One step forward, no matter how many steps we'd taken back.

It was all I had control over.

Up Next: Book 4

I was magnetically attracted to him.

At the moment, for example, I was having an incredibly difficult time pulling my attention from his face. The thick lashes and warm brown eyes, the slope of his nose, how it leaned ever slightly in the same direction of his hair, how that hair fell across his forehead. His lips, how I'd never noticed before how perfect they were or the tiny freckle by his ear. Sometimes, if I was feeling less brave, it would be his hand I studied instead, or his forearm, or all of him at once.

We were texting back and forth as we sat side by side and he laughed at what I'd just sent him. That was another thing—his voice, his chuckle, his big booming laugh—all of them flushed me warm, like sun sweeping out from behind thick clouds.

How could I carry on like normal when things were so not normal anymore? Normal was easy and laid back, normal was friends. Maybe it had been festering inside me for longer than I knew, maybe I'd pushed it down time and again, but there was no hope for that anymore. I could hardly contain it at this point.

But what if he didn't feel the same way? Because I simply couldn't lose him, the thought alone sucked all the joy out of me. Or it would have anyway, if I wasn't bursting, coming apart at the seams, being blown away with it.

Heck, I should just tell him right now. It wouldn't be hard to force out. In fact, it would probably spill out if I opened my mouth just the slightest, on the tip of my tongue as it already was.

I bit my tongue.

Because now was a bad time. I had to be at work in ten minutes.

"I don't have time to bring you home." I pulled my feet down from his lap.

Riah smirked. "I know, I thought maybe you were bringing me with you."

I'd done a lot of that lately. At least when he wasn't already working his real job in Rob Ashby's council office. "That was sort of my plan. Wanna?"

"I think it's my most lucrative hobby. Last Saturday, Mr. P handed me a fifty from the till." He stood and grabbed my keys from the table.

The first time Riah made himself useful at Parrino's, it was because we were all working—Ethan, Stella, and I. He'd come in with his sisters and their friends to eat pizza, but hadn't left with them. Instead, he'd wandered into the kitchen an hour or so before close and started on the dishes.

The three of us worked pretty much every Saturday night and when Riah started complaining about having to spend so much time with his sisters, Ethan told him to stop whining and come with us instead. So he had.

Mr. Parrino simply watched him as he helped out Ethan in the kitchen, picked up the dishes when the dishwasher went on break, slid into the hostess stand when the hostess was dealing with a rather high maintenance customer, and helped Stella and I with drinks and bread when things got crazy.

A few weeks later he did it again, and then again, until it became a regular thing.

We entered in back, directly into the kitchen, where Ethan was wearing a chef's apron and helping out his brother. Eric was a full time cook now that he'd graduated high school, and being the newest of these he got stuck working most of the Saturdays with the rest of us.

I stopped at the time clock and punched in. It was an old mechanical thing that actually punched the time and date with ink. Eric grumbled about it every time it made its satisfying click, since he was the one who had to take it apart and put it back together when it broke down, something that was happening with greater and greater frequency.

Stella breezed through the door as I adjusted my black pencil skirt and smoothed my white blouse. She punched in, kissed me on the cheek, and rushed out past me to the hostess stand. I followed her, and we both peered over Sutton's shoulder to find out what section we had. Sutton mostly hosted, but when Mr. P wasn't there, he was also in charge.

I scanned the tables on his clipboard and noted with a sinking stomach that I'd finally been assigned to the cellar. I hadn't had to serve down there yet, and figured this was because, at least when it came to blood, I had a comparatively weak stomach. But I was long past due.

Stella, along with Carrie and Robby, had the dining room, and Iris was on pizza duty. Pizza duty was what we called the more casual section in the bar, the tables up by the front window, since the menu there was pared down to soup, salad, and pizza.

I sighed and wandered over to the booth where Stella and Robby were prepping. Robby was forming cloth napkins into tulips, something I still hadn't mastered, and Stella was pouring salt. I slumped down next to Stella.

"What's the matter, love?" Robby asked without looking up, his tongue sticking out in concentration.

"She got the cellar," Stella told him.

"I don't get how you can handle the scampering shrimp but not the blood pies."

It wasn't so much blood alone that turned my stomach anymore, I was used to that. It was the smell of it hot. I wrinkled my nose.

"Mmm, scampering shrimp." Stella took the moment to pat her belly in appreciation. The staff called the shrimp scampi scampering shrimp because that was pretty much what it did. It was a tricky plate to get to the table, though thankfully was served in a shallow bowl to make it easier. The shrimp were alive, and frantic at having been thrown onto steaming hot, garlic butter sauce.

Robby looked up, pleased with his napkin creation, and glanced toward the space that led from the back of the dining room into the back of the bar. This opening happened right at the top of the cellar stairs. "At least you get to wait on them." He let out a low whistle. Exactly the kind you heard construction workers letting loose in old movies.

Sutton was leading Sofia and Elbie down the steps. Sofia was the first enemy I made here in Shady, when I unknowingly moved in on her boyfriend. Who later became my boyfriend. And Elbie was a wild who'd come in last year when our new town council opened the place up to any abnormals, not just the pacifists. Because of course Sofia would jump on the wild bandwagon as soon as it came to town.

I groaned, while Robby craned his neck to get a better look at Elbie's butt before it disappeared.

With a sigh, I followed after them down the stone steps. It was a small room, with seven tables and a little bar. Constantine, the bartender down there, glanced up and nodded at me. The lights were low and the candles on the tables sat in red votives, rather than the pure white of the upstairs dining area.

The cellar was generally an easy night, as food was only occasionally ordered. When it was though, it was most often the blood pies. And instead of bread, I had to serve shots, a trio of animal bloods to enjoy before the meal. Constantine always had these ready, and I swept up the tray he'd laid them on.

Bracing myself, I approached their table and forced a smile. "Good evening."

"They sent *you* to serve me?" Sofia let out a laugh, something between cackle and delight.

Ignoring her, I kept to the script. "Have either of you enjoyed the cellar experience before?"

"I have not." Elbie was eyeing the menu with skepticism. Since he'd been raised wild, he was used to his blood fresh from a warm body, as opposed to cooked into a pizza crust.

"Well, here is your Parrino trio." I set the shots between them. "The cold one," Elbie's face twisted in disgust at this, "is polar bear and will cool your body temperature. I've been told it's quite refreshing. The one that's room temp is feline and stirs contentment. The one steaming hot is a special sloth and tortoise mixture that Constantine created just for us, and it should relax you." As if they needed that, vampires. They were cool as cool could be by nature. "Is there anything else I can get you? Aside from a minute to look over the menu?"

Sofia held the steaming shot glass under her nose and took a deep breath in, then waved me away with the flick of a hand.

Also By J Mercer

More of the Shady Woods series

Shady Woods

The Little Wooden Box

Other young adult novels

Triplicity

Perfection and Other Illusive Things

Reviews really do make the world go round. Please let others know what you thought!

Acknowledgments

Truth be told, I should thank every writer I've ever met who's been a part of my journey, as Shady Woods was what I cut my teeth on. Each of you have helped me grow into the writer I am today—a writer who has been able to rewrite these first story from the mess of 120,000 words to the succinct, quick-paced fun they are today.

Thank you to Kat Olestro, Brie Anderson, and Neva and Aubrey Hinsey, for your excitement that pushed me into putting these out in the world in the first place, even after I'd long moved past writing paranormal.

Don't worry, I'll keep writing it for as long as it takes to finish Grace's story (2 more books), and maybe someday I'll come back around for the spinoff that's been in my head for a decade or so. If only there weren't so many other ideas sitting alongside it.

And, of course, always a heartfelt thank you to my readers—just as a tree doesn't make a sound in the forest if there's no one to hear it (no need to argue, you know what I mean), a book doesn't live and breathe if there are no readers to read it.

9 7989 87 256701